Fae's Mate

A Fated Fae Novel

For Lizzie
From
LDaye

Luna Daye

ISBN: 978-1-7396888-1-3

This is a work of fiction. Names, characters, places, and incidents are the product of the author's imagination or are used fictitiously. Any resemblance to actual person, living or dead, events, or locales in entirely coincidental.

Lunadaye@Lunadaye.com

Cover by Sarah (Moonrosesxart)
Map by Luna Daye

Fae's Mate

A Fated Fae Novel

Luna Daye

For those who use books to escape to magical realms, when life gets too tough.

Preface:

Please read before starting your adventure. The Fated Fae series is a work of **adult** fantasy fiction. As such it includes mature themes scenes of a sexual nature, which are described in graphic detail.

A full list of content warnings can be found on my website:
LunaDaye.com

The Humans:

Seki: Japanese/American, black hair, brown eyes, college drop-out, baker/cake shop owner.

Alana: African/American, black hair, brown eyes, librarian, wears glasses, avid reader- especially fantasy.

Amber: Long golden-brown hair, green eyes, beautician, quiet/secretive.

Riley: Male, ginger, green eyes, history teacher, likes tea.

Edith: Blonde hair, brown eyes, at Uni learning to be a vet, likes star signs, but is afraid of the dark.

Sascha: Black hair, green eyes, vegetarian, creative, animal rights activist.

Willow: Blue hair, grey eyes, free Spirit/hippie, stoner, travel blogger.

Alexis: (Prefers Alex) ginger, brown eyes, community support officer, active/fit, loves music.

Mollie: White blonde curls, blue eyes, angry/bitter bar/restaurant owner, short.

Charlotte: curvy, honey blonde, green eyes, nerd/gamer, worked in a supermarket, good at strategy (from games)

Yasmin: Deaf, biracial, brown hair, green eyes, loves to paint and draw.

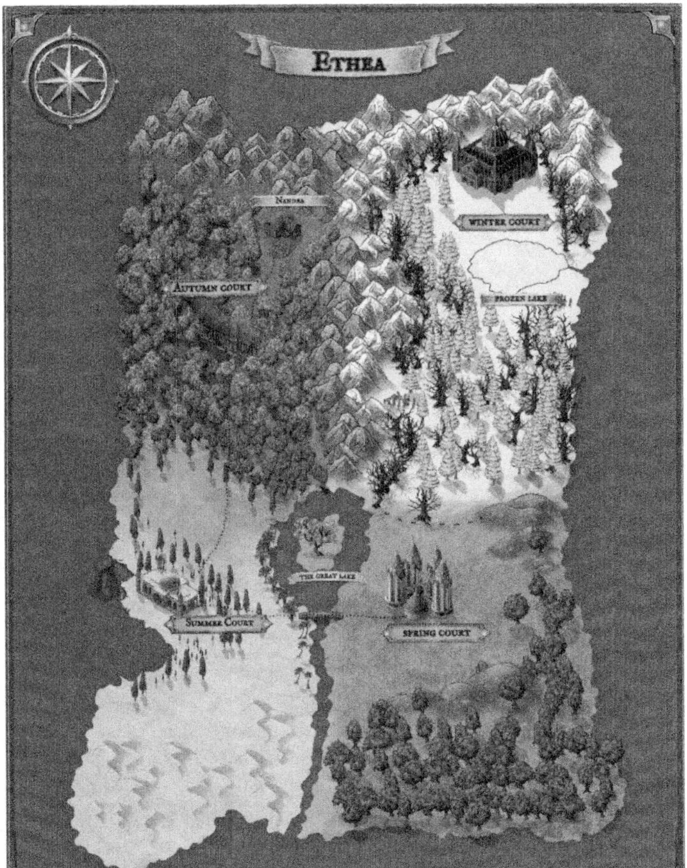
Ethea
Nandra
Winter Court
Autumn Court
Frozen Lake
Summer Court
Spring Court

Chapter 1

Seki

I try not to roll my eyes as the bell above the door dings. My shop has been empty for an hour and I was preparing myself for an early close. I plaster on a fake smile and turn to my customer.

"How can I help?"

"Oh, I'm just looking for a moment." The blonde woman on the other side of the glass counter says.

I've seen her before. She hides her full figure under baggy clothes, is always polite, and always buys more than one cake. I turn off the tap and return to cleaning dishes, sighing heavily as I scrub orange buttercream from a mixing bowl. The Halloween cupcakes I made didn't sell as well as I had hoped they would. Another week of barely turning a profit.

"Okay, I'm ready." My customer calls.

I turn with another fake smile, wiping my wet hands on my apron.

"Can I have two of the Halloween cupcakes, a rocky road and a chocolate brownie please, oh, and a pumpkin spiced latte to go, please?"

"Of course," I reply with thinly veiled sincerity; I just cleaned the coffee maker, now I'll have to do it again.

I push in the coffee and clip the porta filter to the machine, reminding myself that I should probably make small talk. "Do you have anything nice planned for this evening?"

"Oh, me? No, I live on the top floor, so I tend not to get any trick or treaters. I will probably just watch a horror movie."

Nodding politely, I grab a box and fill it with her order, then place it carefully in a paper bag so the buttercream doesn't get smushed. A strange smell fills the air and I wonder for a moment if it's simply the blonde woman's perfume—a light floral fragrance—but as I walk over to froth milk for her latte, the smell intensifies.

The air suddenly feels thick—heavy—like it does in the summer, and I wonder if I left the ovens on again. When I turn to look at my customer, she is looking around curiously, sniffing the air. She must smell it too, and tugs at the neck of her hoodie as if she too feels the intensity of the air.

A weird ringing sound fills the shop, and the air thickens more, becoming almost misty, and as I look around, it shimmers. Am I seeing things?

"What's going o—"

Everything disappears in a blinding flash of white light, and for a moment, I feel nothing. Everything is still, quiet, and calm. As if the entire world is paused. Floating in the nothingness, I feel like I could almost drift away…

But then I hit the ground. *Hard.*

Winded, I stay on my back, eyes closed as I struggle to suck in the air. I didn't initially realise I had been denied it. The surrounding air is earthy and damp, and the ground beneath me is soft and soggy. With a groan, I finally open my eyes. Above me is a vast canopy of red and orange leaves, almost completely blocking out the sun. A rustle sounds beside me and I quickly sit up to look around.

I'm in a forest, though it doesn't look like any forest I have been in before, and I am not alone. Ten feet away is the blonde woman from my shop. Scattered nearby are a handful of others, all sitting up groggily. To my left is a dark-skinned woman with glasses, wearing a paisley shirt. Beside her is another blonde, but younger looking, with big doe like brown eyes. Opposite me, leaning against a tree, is a slender woman with bright blue hair, a big, flared skirt and bangles gracing both her arms.

"Where are we?" the doe eyed blonde asks.

I wait, but no one answers her. I stand and wipe away the fallen leaves clinging to me as best I can. Now that I've had a good look around, the forest seems to stretch further than I can see in every direction. I can hear a babbling brook nearby and birdsong, but no cars. We must be miles from the city. A sob breaks through the quiet. A woman, to my right, with gorgeous long golden-brown curls.

It's then that I notice the bodies on the ground.

I step over to them without alerting the others. I should probably say something, but I don't want to cause a panic. As I draw closer, I see they are both male and unconscious. Not dead, because their chests are rising and falling. One has strawberry-blonde hair, braided like an elf from a fantasy movie, and the other has a halo of black coils. Both are dressed as if they've been to some sort of fair, the kind where people dress up as wizards and hobbits.

As I frown at the two unconscious men, another woman comes to stand beside me.

"Do you know them?" She asks.

I shake my head, then look over at her. This is someone new, a tall woman, with a large set of headphones resting around her neck and ginger hair that is shaved on one side and falls to her jaw in waves on the other.

The dark-skinned woman with glasses joins us and crouches beside the men. She presses her fingers to one of their necks, checking for a pulse, then pushes auburn hair away, revealing a high pointed ear. She scoffs, then reaches for the ear and tries to pull the cosplay extensions off. Except they aren't extensions, but his *actual* ears. The woman stands so quickly that she stumbles back and lands with a thud, pushing up her glasses.

"They're… they're f-fae."

"Fae?" I ask.

"Like, don't step in the mushroom ring, has elemental magic fae?" The blonde from my shop asks.

"I think so." The bespeckled woman replies, somewhat composed now.

A giggle comes from the other side of the two 'fae' men, the blue-haired woman. "I should really stop leaving the house high."

"We need to find something to bind them with and gag them." The woman who discovered their ears declares.

"What?" I ask, in disbelief.

"Well, if they are anything like the fae I have read about, they can't lie, but they can trick you with riddles, so we should just gag them to stop them from talking. Does anyone have anything made of iron?"

"Iron?" the woman with headphones asks.

"Yes, fae are allergic to iron."

I roll my eyes. This is ridiculous.

The ground shakes, a trembling rumble that has everyone frantically looking around for the source. We cluster together instinctually as the thundering gets louder.

"More are coming!" Someone shouts.

"Whatever you do, don't apologise to them, don't offend them, and *don't* agree to any deals!" The dark-skinned woman with glasses commands us all as a dozen horses emerge from the trees, bearing weapon wielding fae riders.

Chapter 2

High Lord

The ripple of magic that shook the palace still vibrates in the air. Luckily, I was already in the stable, making my rounds when it happened, and I was able to assemble a dozen men quickly to follow me into the woods to discover the cause. At first, I had assumed it was Winter Court causing trouble again. It has been a while since their last attack, and another one is due.

But, as we gallop into the clearing, we find a group of strangers. All gathered around my unconscious brother and the youngest Lord from Summer Court. Without having to say a word, my men surround the strangers, spears aimed at them, in a perfect circle. I immediately count ten of them. They're a peculiar lot. One has hair the colour of the ocean, another wears circles of glass in front of her eyes, and they don't *smell* right. Not a single one of them shows any sign of magic, not that it is common for lesser fae…

I study closer; one with orange hair like my brother has her locks cut short, revealing small, curved ears.

Another has her black hair pulled back from her face and bound in a long tail. Her ears are the same. It cannot be…

"You are… human," I remark, my voice more choked than I intend.

"Of course we are." The orange-haired woman scoffs, as if I have stated something stupid. I glare at her, and she casts her eyes back to the ground.

"Tell me how you got here." I demand.

"We don't know," replies a woman with hair the colour of honey. "There was a bright light, then we all just… woke up in the woods."

Fates. Someone cleaved open a portal.

I didn't think there was enough magic left in the realm for that. I search around for any sign of the magic still in the air, but it seems to have dispersed. Leaves rustle to my right and my ears prick up. I turn to where the sound came from and spot another female stepping out from the trees, but upon sighting us, she turns and runs.

With a flick of my head, one of my guards gallops after her. She doesn't get far before he drags her back. She shouts and cries in his firm grip, but her words are strange. When she is pushed into the circle with the others, she makes quick gestures with her hands, looking around. The orange haired female grabs her by the shoulders, then makes hand gestures herself. Are they communicating?

I watch the exchange for a moment, then they both shrug and sigh, turning back to face me. They are all dressed strangely, in clothing that does not belong to any of the four courts. As I survey them more closely, I find a dark-haired female standing to the left of the group. Her black hair is cut short across her brow, then falls in slick straight lines down to her shoulders. She is wearing a white apron, covered in stains—she must be some kind of maid—but when her dark brown eyes meet mine, the world tilts. It takes all my strength not to fall from my horse as gravity shifts beneath me, re-centring around the human woman before me.

Shit

"Bring them back to the palace and pick up my brother and the young Lord."

The group of humans murmurs amongst themselves as we travel back through the forest. It's slow going as they are on foot, and a couple of them are crying. I try to ignore the sound. I don't trust them, I can't, not yet, not until I know where they're from and what they're doing here. As the sun sets, we reach the edge of the woods. The palace comes into view, looming above the trees in all its grandeur.

Oh, how I long to see it full of life and magic again.

Behind me a few of the humans gasp, taking in the sight. Perhaps none of them have seen a palace before. It *is* magnificent; built of dark brown stone from the quarry in the north, topped with deep red wood. Spires twist towards the sky with coloured glass in all the windows, and a wide moat of shimmering azure water surrounds it.

"Take my brother to his room, and the young Lord to a guest room. As for the humans, put them all in one place until I can decide what to do with them. I want guards at all three doors."

"*Yessir.*"

First, I drop my horse off at the stable and ensure he gets an apple, then make my way back through the warm stone walls of the palace to my study. It's no surprise to find my sister sitting in the window seat, awaiting my return.

"That didn't take long," she remarks.

My sister—well, half-sister—lounges on the plump velvet cushions, illuminated by the ebbing sunlight that filters through the colourful window. The light sparkles over her warm, light brown skin and her long, dark, wavy hair. Her mother was a lady of the Summer Court, or so our father told us just before his magic faded.

"We found eleven humans in the woods. Our brother and the young Lord from Summer Court were with them, both unconscious." I say, troubled.

"But… The only way for humans to get here now is through a magic portal."

"I *know*."

"Fates," she breathes, "I didn't think our brother had it in him to cleave one open."

"I don't think he acted alone. The Summer Lord has illusion magic. They must have worked together."

She raises her brow at me, questioning without asking, and I shake my head. My brother hasn't had a vision in months, as far as I know. Fates only know what possessed him to open a portal. It makes sense that he would ask the Summer Lord for help. They've been spending a lot of time together, and illusion magic is predisposed for portal cleaving, but *fates*, they both could've died wielding that much magic.

And *why* use what *could* have been their last kernel of magic to drag eleven humans through the veil?

"Once our brother is conscious again, I'll speak with him. Then we must decide what we are going to do with eleven humans." I say, exasperated.

I don't mention to my sister that I have found my mate.

Chapter 3

Seki

The fae guards escort us through the enormous palace, which oddly seems almost bereft of people. We finally come to a large room at the end of a corridor. When I enter, I realise it's not just a room, but more of a suite. The space we step into is a type of living room, with couches and bookshelves and an enormous stone fireplace, and there is a bathroom and two bedrooms branching off to one side. Once we are all inside, the large oak doors slam shut behind us and the lock clicks. Our group stands close together, no one daring to step away. Strength in numbers, I guess.

"Are you *sure* they're fae?" The only male in our group asks.

"As sure as I can be." The woman with glasses replies.

A flurry of questions ensues, and the poor woman looks overwhelmed.

"Hey, hey!" I bark. "Leave her be. We'll learn who they are and what they want with us soon enough!"

She wanders over to me, arms wrapped around herself. "Thank you."

"No problem," I shrug, "I'm Seki."

"Alana."

"This is pretty mad." I point out.

"You're telling me. I thought Fae were just in folktales and fantasy stories. I never imagined them to be *real*."

"This has to be some sort of group trip," the blue-haired woman adds as she glides over to us, her bangles jangling.

"I don't take drugs," Alana insists.

"Not knowingly. Maybe there was something in the air or water. I know I had a joint just before it happened, but that doesn't normally set me off this bad. I'm Willow, by the way."

I just smile and introduce myself. Could there have been something in the air? The blonde customer and I both seemed to notice the air shift in my shop. Maybe Willow is right, and we all have been drugged somehow. That makes more sense than Fae, anyway.

"So, what's the plan?" The woman with ginger hair asks as she joins our little group. I notice she has multiple piercings in her ears and one through her lip.

"Well, Willow here thinks we are experiencing some sort of mass *trip*, but I don't know. If we have somehow crossed into a magical realm—*fuck*, that sounds crazy—then I guess we have to wait and find out why, then work out how to get back."

"How is she?" Alana asks, nodding her head towards the deaf girl, who lingers close to us, but not quite part of the group.

"Scared shitless." The pierced red-head replies.

"Aren't we all?" I add.

"What are your names?" Alana asks.

"I'm Alexi, but I go by Alex, and she's Yasmin."

"Did any of you feel that weird thrumming when the leader looked at you?" I query.

All of them stare at me for a moment and I wish I had kept quiet.

"No, I mean… when he glared at me for answering his question, I was terrified. Backing down isn't usually my style but, shit…" Alex explains.

"Just me then," I huff.

Looking around, I notice the group has divided up. The four of us have clustered together, and Yasmin stands on her own off to one side. The redheaded man, and the woman from my shop, have joined the woman with the long golden-brown curls—who still looks immaculate, even after hiking through the woods. Off to another corner, in front of a bookshelf, is a black-haired woman, wearing all black and heavy makeup, with a blonde on either side. The blonde with tight bouncy curls looks vicious and is whispering furiously to the dark-haired woman, while the other blonde just stands to one side, looking awkward.

I really should learn everyone's names…

The door unlocks, and the leader walks in, followed by two of his guards. He's not as fearsome now, with his armour removed. I spot a dagger at his side, but other than that, he has discarded his other weapons. The guards are still terrifying, wearing full armour and each carrying a multitude of blades. I swallow the lump in my throat.

When the leader scans the room, his gaze eventually settles on me, and it's like the air is sucked from the room. He holds my stare, his jaw clenched and eyes unreadable for a few moments, then releases me. I draw in a breath.

What the fuck?

The leader stands confidently in front of us all, his arms behind his back. Finally, after taking a deep breath, he addresses us. "You have the right to know what has happened. I have spoken to my brother, who has confirmed he had a hand in opening the portal—"

"Why?" the dark-haired woman by the bookshelf, who is wearing all black, asks.

"Do not interrupt me. I will tell you what there is to be told." He growls. Her eyes fall to the floor. "I will punish my brother for what he has done, as will his accomplice." He scans the silent room, avoiding looking at me this time. "The amount of magic needed to cleave a portal is… vast. It will take some time to gather enough magic to do it again. Until then, you will remain here."

The room erupts. All around comes protests and demands for answers. Behind me, someone cries. I remain silent, watching as the leader glares at the room impatiently. Alex rushes off to Yasmin, signing furiously at her, clearly repeating what has been said.

"Silence!" He roars, and everyone obeys. He glances around the room, again avoiding me. "I will speak to each of you individually, as I wish to know more about the humans now residing in my court. Starting with you." He points a finger in my direction and before I can protest, he turns and paces from the room.

His guards approach me, and Alana grabs my arm. "He can't lie, but don't apologise, and don't make any deals!" She whispers.

I swallow and nod, then follow the guards from the room.

Chapter 4

High Lord

I can feel her behind me, like a beam of sunlight cutting through the trees, warming my skin. Clenching my fists at my side, I try to shrug off the distraction. A human female is my mate?

Ridiculous!

When we enter my study, I walk around to the far side of my desk. I find two glasses and fill them with wine while I wait until the door closes and we are alone. I take a deep breath to steady myself, then turn to her. She waits, small and frightened, just past the threshold.

I offer her a glass, but she shakes her head. "No, thank you."

I tilt my head, confused. She must be thirsty. "It's not poisoned… or glamoured, if that is your concern."

"I… no, I just don't drink alcohol."

"Ah, water then."

"Thank you."

I take an empty glass and allow the rare tingle across my skin, summoning water using my magic. I peek up and see her face filled with awe. It seems odd to me that this minor act should impress her when my ancestors could summon tidal waves. Then I remember that this is likely the first time she has seen magic.

She takes the glass tentatively when I hand it to her, and sips from it slowly. "Sit," I encourage, gesturing to the empty seat in front of my desk.

When she does, I walk around the large wooden table and sit opposite her. Sipping from my glass, I let the silence continue a moment, curiosity stilling my tongue. Now we are alone, I feel able to look upon her without interruption. I take in her silky black hair, her dark wide eyes and pale flawless skin. She is a good foot shorter than me, but I am a tall male, so that is not surprising. I wonder if she feels this tension too? Like a bow string pulled back, ready to loose.

"I wish to know your name," I tell her eventually.

"Seki… what's yours?" she asks, linking her ankles together, sitting up straight.

"A name is a powerful thing," I reply with a smirk. She gave me hers so easily.

"You won't tell me?"

"Not yet." I sip again from my glass. "Tell me, Seki, I would like to know what you do in the human realm."

She considers me for a moment before answering. "Why should I tell you anything?"

My lip twitches into a sly smile, which I hide behind my hand, pretending to rub the stubble along my jaw. "Because I am High Lord of Autumn Court, I expect all my subjects to answer me, should I ask them a question."

"But I'm not one of your subjects. I'm not a fae."

"Yes, but you are currently residing in my court."

"Not by choice," she argues.

"Perhaps not, but you wish for you and your friends to remain safe and protected while you are here, I'm sure." A hollow threat.

"They aren't my friends." She says. I raise an eyebrow at her, her words catching me off guard. "Are all fae friends?"

"I suppose not." I reply, swirling the drink in my glass.

"The same as all humans, are not friends. I've met none of them before today."

Interesting…

"Very well… you may ask me five questions. For each one I answer, you must answer one of mine."

"Like… a deal?"

I nod.

"I was advised not to make a deal with you."

"You may refuse if you wish."

She stares at me silently for a moment, and the anticipation makes my heart falter. "No," she whispers finally.

"Very well. Ask your first question."

Sipping my drink, I wait while she decides what to ask.

"Are you able to lie?"

"Yes," I say with assurance. She frowns at my answer. Clearly, the common misconception amongst humans still exists. I don't elaborate any further.

"Are you allergic to iron?"

I balk. Why do humans always seem to remember that iron is harmful to us? I consider being pedantic; Allergic is not the right term…

"We are not *allergic* to iron, no, but it is harmful."

"How?"

A question falls from my lips before I can stop it.

"Do you wish to hurt me, Seki?" I ask, amused.

"Not yet." There is an edge of defiance in her voice, even as her fingers knit in her lap. Do I make her nervous?

I can't help but chuckle. "Proximity to iron hinders our magic, and injury from iron can be fatal."

She nods her understanding. I sense she wishes to question me further about this, but she only has two questions left. "How long will it take for your brother to regain his magic?"

"I don't know." I answer honestly.

One question left. I wonder if she will use it to ask about the bond between us.

"Do you mean us harm?" She asks, voice cautious.

"No." I answer quickly.

I have no reason to bring harm to the humans unless they reveal themselves to be a threat to me and my court.

"My turn." Seki shifts uncomfortably in her seat, as if I am about to interrogate her. "What do you do in the human realm?"

"Bake." Her one-word answer amuses me. Clearly, she plans to be as evasive as I was.

"Do you have a family?"

Her dark brows knit together at my question, and a flash of uncertainty dances over her perfect face. "Yes," is her only response.

That is not enough information. I want to know if her parents still live, if she has siblings, does she have a mate? Do humans even have mates? The thought of it brings a sudden surge of jealousy, but I stamp it down. I realise she is still too wary of me to give me any decent answers.

So, I decide to keep my questions, for now.

"I appreciate your answers. You may go."

"But you still have two more questions."

"I have three, but I do not wish to ask them yet."

"You asked me if I wish to hurt you… so you only have two left."

"Very well," I grin, happy to be caught out at my own game. "I will ask the final *two* questions when I have something further to ask."

She stares at me, her dark eyes assessing, and I wonder if she regrets entering into a deal with me. Which of the humans knows the danger of making deals with us? Do they know how binding they are? Does Seki know? Does she realise I could ask her any question, at any time and she would have to answer me?

After what feels like a lifetime under her gaze, she slurps the rest of her water, placing the glass on my desk with a little too much force and rises from her seat. "Well then, good day to you, *High Lord*," she seethes, then storms from the room.

I feel both relieved and distressed at her absence. Even the way she spits my title with contempt fills me with something I haven't felt in a long time. Arousal. I'm grateful to be sitting behind my desk, as it hides the evidence.

"Bring me another!" I bark at the guards beyond my door, then gulp the rest of the wine from the glass.

Fates, what a nightmare.

Chapter 5

Seki

When I return to the suite, everyone is still in the same groups as before. I am suddenly uncomfortable when everyone's gaze flicks to me, so I quickly shuffle over to the group I was with earlier, who have taken to sitting in a small circle close to the fireplace. Slumping down on a cushion, I let out a sigh, grateful to be free of the thick vibrating air that seems to surround me whenever I am around the High Lord.

"So… how'd it go?" Alana asks me nervously.

"Well, apparently, they *can* lie. But you were right about iron."

"We already asked around," Alex explains. "No one has anything made of iron."

The guards darken the doorway, having followed me back, and point to the curvy blonde from my shop. She bites her lip, then walks slowly towards them. Then the doors close and lock behind her.

"Do we know everyone else's names?" I ask.

Alex nods, "The guy is Riley, the woman with the

long curls that keeps crying, is Amber—she's been throwing up for the last half hour. The lady that went with the guards is Charlotte. Then the three in the corner there," she jerks her head in their direction, "are Mollie with the curls, Edith with the long blonde hair, and Sascha is dressed all in black."

I nod, trying to commit the names to my memory.

"Did you find out *his*?" Alana asks.

"No, he wouldn't tell me. He said names are *powerful*. So, I guess we just call him High Lord for now," I crinkle my nose.

"Powerful, *how*?"

"I'm not sure."

"Did you give him yours?" Alana pushes.

All I can do is nod, then shrug, not able to work out how names hold any power. I spend the next few minutes staring into the fire, watching the flames crackle as I try to guess what his name might be. I'm running through some posh 'British lord' sounding names like Humphrey and Albert when Charlotte returns. Behind her are a handful of people, all with slightly pointed ears, dressed in simple clothing and following her with armfuls of blankets and cushions. I imagine they are servants, then. They place all the bedding in the center of the room, then scurry away without saying a word to us.

"I asked the High Lord about sleeping arrangements," Charlotte begins, as she approaches our group. "He said he would arrange accommodation tomorrow, but for tonight we should all sleep in here."

"Slumber party!" Willow remarks cheerfully, and I roll my eyes.

Just as I remember the two bedrooms attached to the main room, I see Mollie and Sascha, abandoning poor Edith, rush for one room, while Amber and Riley sneak into the other.

"Do you suppose they're hooking up?" Alana

wonders out loud.

I shake my head. "Doubt it, but they seem to have bonded over their shared kidnap… human-nap?"

Beside me, Yasmin is signing frantically to Alex, who then signs back and rests a hand on Yasmin's shoulder. Alex turns to me. "Yaz is worried that if something happens in the night, she won't be able to hear it, and has asked me to sleep beside her. Will you take the other side?"

"Sure."

I grab us all some pillows and blankets and we arrange them close to the fire, but not so close that we risk setting fire to ourselves in the middle of the night. Edith is the next person called from the room, and I wonder if the High Lord will speak to all of us tonight, or if Edith will be the last and he will speak to the rest tomorrow.

The others settle down beside me. Yaz, then Alex and Alana, then Willow at the end. Charlotte has snuggled up on one of the couches and when Edith returns, she does the same. No one else is called away and a wary sort of quiet falls over the group. In the distance muffled crying taints the air, Amber I think, in one of the bedrooms—she's really having a tough time with all this. To be honest, I'm surprised more people *aren't* freaking out. Who knows how long we are going to be trapped here? Just as the crying stops, Willow starts snoring and I roll my eyes. I will not get any sleep.

Staring up at the elaborately carved ceiling, my mind wanders back to the High Lord, and I wonder what sort of questions he will ask me next time we speak. I wrack my brain trying to figure out what I should keep secret about myself, and what would be harmless to tell him. Feeling like I should suspect *every* question, my brain tangles itself up, attempting to guess what he will want to know, and why.

As I drift off to sleep, all I can think about is the way his brown eyes cut right into my soul, and the feeling of the heavy vibrating air between us.

Chapter 6

High Lord

I groan as the first rays of sun bleed through the window. I've barely slept, my sleep constantly disrupted with images of Seki. Unable to shake her from my thoughts, and my cock has been agonisingly hard all night, despite failed attempts to alleviate myself. Thrice.

With a huff, I throw back my bedding and ready myself for the day. I only spoke with three of the humans yesterday and plan to speak with the other eight today, which will probably take up most of my morning. I try to think of an excuse to call upon Seki again but come up short.

As I make my way through the palace, I realise I will need to feed the humans. A wave of anxiety washes over me as I contemplate feeding eleven more mouths. I may have to call on Summer Court for aid. I *am* in this predicament because of one of theirs, after all.

When I enter the kitchen, the servants all bow to me before swiftly resuming their work. I tell them what to prepare, and that today, it is to be served in the dining hall, as opposed to the various quarters that are resided in by courtiers. Of the three high fae living in the palace, myself included, one will probably not deign to eat with the humans, while the other is in the dungeon below.

It isn't long before the long oak table is dressed and laden with plates. I sit at the head of the table alone, as my sister—as I predicted—has chosen not to join us, and await the humans. I hear them before I see them, chattering loudly amongst themselves, and my chest tightens with anticipation. Though I don't show it, instead I remain sat perched in my high-back chair, maintaining a nonchalant composure.

As the human's filter into the room, they pause as they behold the breakfast I have laid out for them. I gesture for them to join me.

"Well, I'm starving!" Remarks the blue-haired female who waltzes over to the table, jangling across the room, then perches halfway along it and starts loading her plate.

It doesn't take long for the others to follow suit. I notice that the two chairs on either side of me remain empty, no one daring to sit so close. Not even Seki, who has chosen to sit the furthest from me. Disappointment gnaws at my gut. Sipping from my wineglass, I watch them all silently. My elbow rests on the table, my chin propped up by my fist. When the chatter dies down, replaced by moans of delight as they eat, I decide to address them.

"Breakfast will be served here each morning; you do not need to all attend together if you do not wish to." No one speaks, so I continue. "I will speak with the rest of you throughout the morning, then this afternoon I will arrange your accommodation."

A few murmurs skitter through the group, but they are not meant for my ears. As I wait for silence to fall again, I dare a glance at Seki. She does not look my way, but focuses on the food on her plate. As soon as my gaze falls upon her, my skin heats, and the surrounding air thickens, so I quickly look away. I need to get some fresh air.

"I will leave you to your food," I declare, rising from my seat and heading for the door.

"Wait," someone calls behind me. When I turn, the blonde, curly haired female holds my gaze as the others watch her cautiously. I have not spoken with this one, so I do not yet know her name.

"Do you mean to say we are free to go wherever we want?" She asks softly.

I consider her words for a moment, glancing around at the group of humans, who now all watch me curiously. I should bargain with her for the question, but it is too early, and the humans have not yet learned our ways.

"I don't see why not; you are not my prisoners. I would prefer you stick together this morning, so I may speak with each of you, but after that… go where you wish within the palace and its grounds. If there is somewhere you are not to be, you will find the way locked."

Before anyone else can ask another question, I stalk from the room, not daring to glance at Seki for a second time.

Chapter 7

Seki

The High Lord calls on Willow first after we return to the suite we are all staying in for the time being. I'm curious to see what accommodations he has in mind, but I guess I will just have to wait until this afternoon.

Alana sits beside me, having pulled an armful of books from the shelves, and is now surrounded by them, flicking through the pages. Whatever she's searching for seems to have piqued Riley's interest too, as he and Amber join us by the fire. I haven't heard Amber say a word since she sat down. She just sniffs occasionally, her gaze cloudy as if she is deep in thought.

Alex sits to the other side of me, signing casually to Yasmin, and they occasionally laugh. The two have been almost inseparable. Charlotte sits with us too, nibbling on a weird-looking cookie she swiped from the breakfast table, and I sit alone, which suits me just fine.

I watch the flames flickering in the fire and contemplate my being here. Did time pause when we left the human realm? When we return, will it be to the exact moment we left? Or is time passing by without us? The electric bill for my shop will be through the roof, and my mother will be furious at not being able to reach me. Even if she does only ever call to ask when I'm going to give up on the shop and go back into the education system so that I can 'get a proper job'.

Bangles jangling alerts us that Willow has returned, and the guards point to Yasmin. Alex rises with her and insists they go to see the High Lord together, and both leave the room. This time, when the door closes, it doesn't lock. I bet the guards are still standing on the other side of it, though.

Willow slumps down onto a cushion beside me, her oversized skirt fluttering. "So, what part of Asia are you from?"

I cringe and stifle a groan. "My mom is Japanese, my dad was American, if that's what you mean?"

"Oh cool! Do you speak Japanese?"

"No," I sigh, "I also don't like sushi, or sake, and I don't know any martial arts," I huff.

"Shit… I'm sorry, I didn't mean—" Willow stammers, face flushed.

"It's fine," I grumble. It's not the first time someone has asked me these types of questions just because I look like an anime character.

"No… it's not, that was… look, I'm sorry. Can we start over?"

"Sure," I shrug.

"I only asked, because I spent time in Asia last year. I'm a travel blogger."

"That sounds fun."

"It is, I can't stay in one place too long or I go stir crazy!"

I nod, still staring at the fire.

"I saw you were wearing an apron. Are you some kind of chef?"

"A baker, I own a cake shop on ninth."

"Oh, the one with the rose gold sign?"

"Yeah," I turn to her, "How'd you know that?"

"I live just down the block. I was actually heading to your shop to get cake—because I had the munchies—when I got sucked into that portal thingy."

"So… you were nearby when the portal opened?"

"Yeah… I guess why?"

I don't answer her, instead I turn to Alana.

"Hey, where were you when you were dragged here?"

"At work," she answers, raising a brow.

"Where do you work?"

"In a bookstore… why?"

My stomach does a flip. "The bookstore on ninth, next to a cake shop?"

"Yeah…"

I focus on Riley. "Where were you?"

The cogs turn behind his eyes, and realisation crosses his face as he answers. "I was driving home from work… I was driving down ninth… past the bookstore."

"So, we were all in close proximity when the portal opened?"

"I think so. Charlotte was in my shop, we should ask the others…"

As it turns out, I'm right.

Edith was in the bookstore where Alana works. Mollie was stock taking in the restaurant she owns, on the *other* side of the bookstore, and Amber was at home, in her apartment on the other side of the street. Sascha was in the alley between the bookstore and Mollie's restaurant, tagging the wall, much to Mollie's horror. When Alex and Yasmin return—and Sascha is summoned, halting her argument with a furious Mollie—we ask them. They were nearby too; Alex was also at home, and lives three storeys above Amber, while

Yasmin was in the coffee shop on the side of the street opposite to my shop. The one with the nasty 'cook from frozen' cakes.

"Do you think we should tell the High Lord?" Alana asks.

"Why?" I reply.

She shrugs, "I don't know. I assumed we were from all over, but we were within a block from each other. I guess that might be relevant when they send us back."

I consider her words for a minute. I had also assumed they plucked us from all over the place, but I suppose one big portal rather than a few small ones makes more sense—as much as fae and portals can make any sense.

"No, I don't think we should, not until they confirm we *are* going back."

"You think they might not send us home?" Amber asks, voice wavering, like she might burst into tears again.

"The High Lord said it took a huge amount of magic to bring us here in the first place, and that it would take time to gather that much again. What if they can't?" I say, as kindly as I can.

Amber's lip wobbles, and a tear rolls down her cheek. Riley grips her knee. "They have to send us back. We have lives, they can't *keep* us here." Riley seethes.

"I know," I agree, "But we don't even know why we were brought here."

I decide there and then that it is down to me to get the truth from the High Lord.

Chapter 8

High Lord

My morning drags as I speak to the remaining humans. None of them tell me anything useful and I wonder if I am asking the wrong questions, but it is more likely that I am simply distracted, unable to remove Seki from my thoughts.

The last of the humans leaves my study, the one who is always weeping, Amber, and I release a sigh. None of them seem to know why they were pulled through the portal, and when I spoke to my brother yesterday, he had only just regained consciousness and could only nod, agreeing he'd had something to do with it. I have no other option but to speak with him again, despite how furious I am.

The corridor that leads down to the dungeon is cold and damp. The metallic taste of iron stings the inside of my mouth as I approach. My footsteps echo as I descend the steps into the darkness. Only small pools of light flicker, gifted by the occasional candle.

When I round the corner, my brother is already

standing, as close to the iron grill as he dares. He looks like shit, not surprisingly, considering how much magic he channelled yesterday.

"I don't understand… when I woke yesterday, I was in my chambers… now I am here…" He manages breathlessly.

I sigh, full of exasperation. "You admitted to cleaving a portal."

His auburn brows furrow. "That *doesn't* explain why I am in an iron cell."

"You tore a rift in the veil, one that could have remained open for all you knew. You *risked* the Summer Lord's life. Both of you channelled more magic than either of you could handle. You could have killed yourselves! I can't, for my magic, fathom why." I recompose myself, anger running rampant at his carelessness.

My brother takes a staggered breath, running a hand through his long auburn hair. I know that look on his face; he is considering lying to me. I wait to rip into him, but he whispers,

"For her."

I frown, tilting my head in a silent question.

"My mate… I have been having visions of her for *weeks* now… I knew she wasn't fae, and the only way to meet her was to bring her through a portal. So… I waited for Samhain, when the veil is thinnest, and cleaved the portal… for her."

I did not know he was having visions still. I thought they had faded.

I pace back and forth before his cell. "That doesn't justify what you did. Tell me which one you believe to be your mate." I demand.

He balks. "Which one?"

I stop pacing and nod, bristling at his question; has the iron weakened him so much already?

"You pulled eleven humans through the veil, one male and ten female, you said *her*, so I assume your mate is female. I wish to know which one you believe is yours."

"I… I only meant to pull *her* through…"

"Well, you pulled through nearly a dozen that I must now feed and clothe and protect! Tell me which one you risked war, and your *life* for."

He looks down at the straw scattered floor, unable to meet my fury, and shakes his head. "If I tell you, you will keep her from me."

That surprises me. Will I? I only want to know so I may speak with her again, see if she had any sort of inkling that she was mated to a fae, or if any of the humans even know what that means.

"Please brother, you cannot keep me from my mate," he pleads desperately.

"Oh, I *can*!" I seethe, I will not reward his behaviour by allowing him to meet her.

"I beg you, you don't know what it is like to see her, to know she exists and not be able to claim her!"

Don't I?

"I know what I did was foolish, but if you knew, *knew*, that your mate was real, that you could meet her, you would have risked your life for her too!"

The desperation in his voice carves into my heart. He's right, but I can't tell him that. It has been less than a day since I met my mate, *my* Seki, and already I know I would risk my life for her.

"You risked too much to bring her here, broke far too many rules. For that, you will spend a month down here to atone—"

"No!—"

"Yes, brother, a month, because fates know it will take longer than that for the Summer Lord's magic to return, if it ever returns, and for us to have any hopes of sending them back."

"You can't… send them back."

"Believe me, I can, and I will," I confirm. "You tore eleven humans from their homes, from their lives, their families—"

"I didn't mean to!"

The distress in his voices softens my heart to his plight a fraction. "I know you didn't. That is why I am *only* sentencing you for a month. Perhaps you can see your mate, if she is still here, and wishes to see you, when thirty days are up."

"Brother please," he steps closer to the bars, wincing as he does, "I beg you, do not keep us apart, I have waited, I, I… please."

I shake my head. "My mind is made up."

"Tay—"

"*Don't*," I warn, "Don't you dare use my name after what you have done."

I turn away and almost reach the corner before a hiss fills the air. My brother cries out as the flesh on his hands meets iron.

"Brother, please!" he begs, rattling the bars of his cell.

I keep walking.

"Brother… PLEASE!"

His screaming becomes less audible the farther up the steep stone steps I climb. When I reach the top and close the door, even my fae hearing can no longer hear him. My stomach churns and knots, but he cannot go unpunished. His actions could have caused a war: if the Summer Lord had died, his brother would have sought revenge. It's bad enough that the Lord of the Winter Court sends his wraiths across the border without going to war with Summer Court as well.

And if the portal had stayed open, it could have caused a war with the humans and their iron weapons.

I swallow the lump in my throat and steel my resolve, heading down the hall, ready to deal with the next order of business: finding accommodation for the humans now under my care.

Chapter 9

Seki

It's mid-afternoon before the High Lord comes to take us to our 'accommodation'. I breathe a sigh of relief at the prospect of getting some time to myself. Between Alana and Riley repeating half of what they read in their books, and Willow chewing my ear off about her travels, I'm exhausted.

When he enters the room, his gaze drifts over the group, until he finds me, then his stare remains on me for so long I feel myself blush and avert my eyes. *What the fuck is wrong with me?*

"I assumed you would wish to stay close to one another, so I have arranged for you to stay in the south wing. Nine rooms have been prepared, two of which are more than suitable for two."

Beside me, Alex signs rapidly to Yasmin, who nods quickly, signs something back and grabs the redhead by the arm.

"We'll take one of the double rooms," Alex announces.

"Us too," Riley adds, smiling at Amber. Maybe they are hooking up.

"Then it is decided. Follow me."

Without checking to see if we are in tow, the High Lord strides from the room.

Like a flock of sheep, we amble through the palace, past oak doors, both open and closed. The walls are lined with tapestries and sconces that hold fat candles. The palace is a warren, and by the time we draw to a stop, I am completely lost.

"Here we are," announces the High Lord. "the first two rooms on the right are the larger rooms, for those of you who will be sharing. Please make yourselves comfortable. I will have the evening meal served at sunset."

With that, he stands to one side and allows everyone to pick a room. I scurry past him, avoiding eye contact, aware of his gaze following me, until I reach the end of the corridor and slip into the last room on the left. After slamming the door shut, I take in my surroundings and stifle a gasp. The room is much more opulent than I imagined; airy and spacious, even though the walls are made of stone, and the furniture is a rich dark wood. A four-poster bed stands to my right, draped in dark green velvet with golden fringe and tassels, and beyond it is a doorway that I assume leads to a bathroom. On the opposite wall is a fireplace with a huge fur rug in front of it. The far wall is home to two stained glass double doors that beckon me. Padding over, I push them open and step onto a wooden balcony. The view takes my breath away. Forest stretches out in front of me, a patchwork of red, orange, and yellow. Beyond the trees, I spot snow-capped mountains, and the balcony is so high that the air is cool and crisp.

Footsteps behind me jolt me from my appreciation with a squeal.

"I did not mean to startle you," the High Lord explains. "I only came to check that your room was to your liking."

As I turn, he steps out onto the balcony, and though it is big enough for a small party, it suddenly feels small and cramped. The air once again feels thick and heavy, and that peculiar tightness in my chest returns. I face the forest, sucking in the cool autumn air.

When he comes to stand beside me, his arms folded, resting on the balcony railing, I realise I haven't said a word.

"I'm grateful for the room, its generous of you to put us all up like this."

I see him nod slowly in my peripheral, agreeing with me and I try not to scoff. I wonder if he is thinking about what questions to ask me now that we are alone again, and my pulse quickens.

"The view is beautiful," I continue, only because it is preferable to silence.

"I'm very fond of it."

I take a deep breath, then turn to face him. He's watching me intently and I can't look away. By the light of the setting sun, he looks… handsome. His hair—which I previously thought was a light brown—looks more golden and hangs past his broad shoulders in soft waves. I have the strangest urge to stoke it. His bizarre clothing fits him perfectly, making the most of his physique. When I look back up at his face, as he is a good foot taller than me, I notice his eyes aren't *just* brown either; they are a fascinating chestnut colour, with hints of red. I swallow and look away, feeling weirdly flustered.

"You have spoken to all of us now."

"I have."

"And you are no closer to figuring out why we were brought here," I state.

"That sounds like a question."

I swear I can hear him smirk.

"No."

"Good, because I haven't asked you what I am owed yet."

"Ask away," I challenge, with more conviction than I feel.

"Hmm, not yet."

I don't understand what he is waiting for. He has me alone. Surely, he could ask anything. I release a huff, eager to ask him more questions, but… I don't want him to have any more to hold over my head… *Fuck it.*

"I have more questions," I declare.

"Interesting."

He studies me for a moment, and I feel my stupid cheeks flush again.

"You may ask as many questions as you wish. But for each one you ask of me; I may ask two of you."

"No."

When he raises an eyebrow at me, I try to summon the courage to counter him.

"A question for a question."

He considers me for a moment, before the corner of his mouth curls up. Why do I find that so mesmerising?

"I agree."

I take a deep breath before asking my first question.

"Do you know why we were brought here?"

"Yes."

I huff at his one-word answer.

"Why?"

"Because my brother and his accomplice cleaved a portal."

"I know that already."

"Then perhaps you should not have wasted a question asking me."

"Ugh, this is pointless! You're never going to give

me a straight answer!"

He chuckles, and the sound both infuriates me, and sets my stomach fluttering.

"You need to phrase your questions better."

"Fine. Why did your brother pull us through the portal?"

Silence stretches between us as he considers his answer, a frown on his face.

"Because he believes one of you to be his mate."

I open my mouth, a plethora of questions on my tongue; what is a mate? Who does his brother think is his? Why pull all of us through? But I promptly close it, deciding to ask the first question I thought of, hoping for a definitive answer.

"What is a mate?"

"Something you humans clearly don't have."

I throw up my hands in exasperation. There is a strange look in the High Lord's eye, and I can't stop myself from blurting—"Why won't you give me a straight answer?"

"Because information, much like names, Seki," the way he practically purrs my name releases butterflies in my chest, "is powerful."

If that is the case, I am through asking questions. I'm never going to get a straight answer, and I don't want to give this fae prick any more *power*.

"I have no more questions." I tell him, crossing my arms and looking away.

"Good, my turn."

I refuse to meet his gaze.

"You truly don't know what a mate is?"

I want to simply say 'no', but I'm feeling petulant.

"I don't know."

He pauses, waiting for me to elaborate, but I don't. I just stare at the sunset.

"What do you mean you don't know?" he asks, and

there is a tone of irritation in his voice.

"I mean, *I don't know*."

"Seki—"

"Frustrating isn't it! Not being able to get a straight answer! Now you know how it feels!" I snarl at him.

"Seki, what do you know about fae mates?"

"Nothing."

Clenching my jaw to stop myself from yelling at him, I keep my gaze on the horizon. The sun has now set, but the sky is still streaked with orange and pink.

With what I can only describe as a growl, I hear him stomp away, slamming the door behind him. Released of the strange tension that envelopes me whenever he is near, I feel an odd chill now that he is gone. I glare at the door none the less.

Infuriating Fae prick.

Why couldn't he have just answered my questions? I would have gladly answered his, but no, he insisted on his stupid deal, and twisting his answers so that he didn't actually tell me anything. Still seething, I storm down to the dining hall, but when I enter, my rage disappears like the air released from a popped balloon.

The High Lord isn't there.

Chapter 10

High Lord

I am a coward. The most cowardly High Lord that ever ruled over Autumn Court… perhaps all the courts in the history of the Fae. Last night I did not eat with humans so that I could avoid Seki. This morning I did the same. Instead, I ate in my chambers, like a fates damned *coward*.

How has this human woman already gotten under my skin? Yesterday was a nightmare; I didn't mean for things to get so… twisted. I am reluctant to tell her anything through fear of frightening or offending her, but my avoidance only angers her and pushes her away. No matter what I do, it is wrong. Perhaps I should answer her questions more concisely, but I know how dangerous that could be, even if she does not. Yet surely, if Seki is my mate, she is worth the risk.

I huff with frustration, leave my chambers, and head for my study. Maybe I should speak with each of the humans again to try to determine which one is my brother's mate. I need to know if she feels the bond… if

Seki does. My feet, it seems, have other ideas, and before I realise what I have done, I am in the south wing, at the start of the hall where the human's rooms are.

I guess I'm speaking to Seki first.

Straightening my tunic and smoothing down my hair, I make my way to the end of the corridor. Once outside Seki's room, I take a deep breath before knocking gently.

"She's not there," a hostile voice informs from behind me.

Turning, I find it to be the redhead; Alexis. The tall female leans against the wall, her arms crossed. She has an air to her, like she revels in a fight.

"I wish to know where she is."

Alexis glares at me, clearly not wishing to answer me.

"Tell me," I demand, pouring every ounce of authority I can into my voice.

I watch as the red head bristles.

"She went for a walk."

"There now, that wasn't so hard." I snap, before turning and stalking back down the hall.

Now that I have made my mind up to speak to Seki, I can focus on nothing else. As I pace through the palace in search of her, I find three humans, two female and the male, sat in the library. I am about to ask them if they have seen her, when I hear female voices talking further down the hall. I follow the sound, but as I near, I realise neither of the voices belong to my mate. Rounding the corner, I find Willow, the one with the blue hair who jangles when she walks, and the one with tight blonde curls that always seems angry, sat in the drawing room, discussing something—I don't care what.

When I peer into the room, they stop talking abruptly. I am about to ask if they have seen Seki—etiquette be damned—when a female with shoulder length black hair passes by the window behind them. Ignoring their confusion, I hasten away and head out into the gardens. My boots thump along the paving as I pace along the pathways trying to catch sight of Seki again and I am filled with a strange sort of desperation to find her.

Eventually I see her walk past a maple tree, and I quicken my steps to catch up to her.

"Seki!" I call out when I am close enough.

She turns, and when she discovers who called her name, she rolls her eyes.

"Great, the High Lord has come to interrogate me again," she grumbles.

She is still angry then. The thought of it hurts me. I know we did not part on good terms last night, but she seems unhappy to see me. Yet when I look at her, I am reminded of witnessing the sunrise for the first time.

"No interrogations today," I confirm.

"Hmm."

She continues walking, and I follow alongside her. Silently, we pass through a wide stone archway that leads into a vegetable garden.

"I've never seen so many pumpkins!" She exclaims.

"I didn't know pumpkins existed in the human realm."

"They do. My mother makes the best pumpkin katsu."

"Cat-zoo?"

She giggles at my misunderstanding but smiles when she explains.

"Kah-tzu. It's mashed up pumpkin, coated in egg and seasoned breadcrumbs, deep fried and served with cur—a spicy sauce and usually rice."

"Ahh." I understand *most* of what she has said.

I can't help but smile when I realise it is the first time she has freely told me something. "Seki… when we spoke yesterday… the conversation did not go as I had intended."

She raises an eyebrow at me as she glances my way, but she keeps walking without responding, so I continue.

"Fae don't apologise. It puts the person apologising in debt to the person receiving the apology… But if we did… I would."

"I cannot imagine you apologising," she tells me. "I'm curious what that would sound like."

It is not quite a question, but I answer anyway. "I would tell you I am sorry for insisting we make a deal, for questions to pass between us, and for not answering your questions fully."

"Hmm, that's a terrible apology. I wouldn't have accepted anyway, and you would have been in my debt for no reason."

Her tone is teasing, but I'm uncertain if she jests. When I frown at her, wondering how I could improve my apology, she glances at me, and a soft chuckle escapes her lips.

"Ask your questions again. I will answer them fully," I beseech, suddenly eager to redeem myself.

"No deal?"

"No deal," I confirm.

She sighs and sits on a bench at the far end of the vegetable rows.

"Why did your brother drag us through the portal?"

"What I told you last night was the truth," I begin as I sit beside her. My thigh brushes hers, sending a pulse of energy through me. I hope she doesn't notice when I jerk my leg away. "He believes one of you to be his mate. I think he intended to only pull through one of you."

"Do you know which of us it is?"

"No, he wouldn't tell me."

"Where is he now?"

"Below the palace, in the dungeon. I have sentenced him to a month down there for what he did."

She frowns at me.

"If he can open a portal, surely he will just… portal out."

I shake my head. "He used nearly all of his magic to cleave that portal. That's why you found him unconscious. He'll not be able to open another for a while. Besides, the cells are lined with iron."

"And iron… dampens magic?"

I nod.

With another sigh, she tucks her hair behind her short-rounded ear. I am envious of her fingers, and wish it were mine that smooth her inky strands. Silence stretches between us for a moment, as Seki looks down at her hands, which are folded in her lap. I notice she is wearing strange mottled blue trousers that cling to her legs. Her chequered shoes remind me of a chessboard, and she wears a long sleeve shirt, with an unfamiliar bird inked into the fabric. I have never seen a woman dressed in such a way and I am reminded that I need to find the humans attire.

"And what about mates? What are they?"

I'm not sure how much I should tell her… "Humans don't have them?"

Asking a question makes my insides feel uncomfortable, but I *must* know.

"I… I don't know if it is the same thing… some humans believe in *soulmates*… one person who they are destined to meet and be with."

"It doesn't sound like you believe that," I comment, my voice little more than a whisper. Her *soulmates* do not sound the same, but they are similar.

"If they exist, I haven't found mine yet," she shrugs.

A wave of joy surges through me. My Seki does not already have a mate. It is good to have that confirmed.

"Are your fae mates the same thing?"

"No, not quite, they—"

"Seki?!" someone shouts, and we both look up.

Charlotte, the human with a much rounder body than the rest of the females, and hair the colour of honey, appears in the stone archway.

"Oh! There you are! Alana has—" she halts when she notices me, and stumbles over her words, "Alana… um… Alana was looking for you."

To my disappointment Seki stands and heads towards Charlotte. She is halfway along the row of pumpkins before she turns back to me.

"Thank you. I enjoy our conversations a lot more when there are no deals involved."

She smiles at me then, and it is lovely to behold. All I can do is smile back and bow my head. Any words I may have had are now forgotten. When she reaches Charlotte, they link arms and begin whispering quickly. Only a few seconds later, she disappears out of sight, and the day seems darker for it.

Rising from the bench, I repeat our conversation in my head. Seki doesn't know about mates or the mating bond. Although I am pleased that she does not already have a mate back in the human realm, it worries me she does not know the true meaning of being mated to a fae. My thoughts spin in circles as I make my way back to the palace, while I consider how much I should tell her.

Shaking my head to focus my thoughts, I seek my sister; she has an entire chamber filled with garments I have never seen her wear. That seems like the best place to start in my search for some clothing for the humans. Despite my best efforts, all I can think about is how beautiful Seki will look, clothed in Autumn Court finery.

Chapter 11

Seki

My skin still feels too tight as Charlotte leads me through the palace. The sensation is fading the further I get from the High Lord, but I still feel annoyingly flustered.

"What was that all about?" Charlotte asks me.

"I'll tell you when we get to the others."

She nods and we continue towards the library. I need a few more minutes to get my thoughts straight. I feel like I finally got some solid answers out of the High Lord, but I still don't feel any closer to knowing how we got here. And I still don't know how the whole 'mates' thing works. How am I supposed to figure out who his brother's mate is? *And why does my heart always race when I am around him?*

Charlotte and I weave through the downstairs corridors until we reach the library. I'm glad she seems to know her way around already, because I sure don't. I had only seen the library briefly when I passed it this morning, and as we enter, the grandeur of it hits me.

Books have never really been my thing, but it is a sight for sure. The room is two storeys high, with a huge stained-glass window at the back, dappling the entire room in rainbows, like the inside of a kaleidoscope. Every wall is lined top to bottom with books, and ladders on rollers are propped up against the shelves at intervals. Velvet and leather couches covered with cushions, and fancy wooden desks topped with candelabra are scattered about the room.

"Seki! Over here!" Calls Alana, who is sitting on the floor amidst a pile of cushions and books.

Riley is sat beside her, his nose firmly planted in the book in his hands. Beside him sits Amber, who is braiding Willow's hair.

"Look what I found."

She spins a comprehensive book towards me and, sprawled across both pages, is a beautifully drawn map. It's a wonky circle—an island—divided into four territories. A mountain range stretches along the entire north coast, and there are several large forests and two great lakes, one in the northeast, and one in the south.

"Ethea…" I read the calligraphy name that swirls along the top of the page. "That's the name of the fae realm?"

"I assume so, look—" she points to the north-west corner, "that's the autumn palace, that's where we are. I can't see a gauge for the size of the island, but… its split into the four seasons; Spring, Summer, Autumn, Winter… This book explains about each of the courts. It turns out they are in some sort of perpetual state… like is it always autumn here, always springtime in the Spring Court and so on."

She explains the climate and brief history for each as I scan the map in front of me. The Winter Court looks almost entirely cut off, the mountains to the north reaching down through the border between Autumn and

Winter. There is a small opening between Winter and Spring, running from the edge of a forest in the middle, to the east coast.

"I'm not sure if any of this helps, but… I figured, at least it's nice to know where we are." Alana explains.

"Have you found anything on magic yet?" I ask, "Where it comes from? Who has it? How its… channelled? The High Lord made it sound like there was a limit to how much a fae could use."

Alana shakes her head. "No, but I'll keep looking."

"He said they need to 'gather' more magic to re-open the portal," Charlotte confirms.

"And earlier he told me that his brother used so much… that it rendered him unconscious."

"But there were two unconscious Fae in the woods. Who was the other one?"

I'd forgotten that, and shrug. I wonder if the second fae had just been assisting the High Lord's brother, or if they had also sought to drag through a 'mate'.

"What else did the High Lord say to you?" Alana questions me.

"Well, it turns out his brother opened the portal because he thinks one is us is his *mate*."

"Mate?"

"Yeah… I don't suppose you have found anything on mates in your research?"

"Nope."

"You mean like soulmates?" Riley asks with a scoff, finally lifting his head from his book.

"I don't think so. He didn't finish telling me, but I feel it's a big deal if his brother was willing to risk so much to drag his here."

"You don't believe in soulmates Riley?" Amber asks, as she deftly weaves Willow's blue locks.

"No, I think sometimes you're lucky and find someone decent, but destined to be with one person, preordained by fate or whatever… no."

"I think it's nice to believe that there is someone out there who is perfect for you." Alana says with a wistful grin.

"You've been reading too many fairy tales!" Riley teases.

A ripple of laughter passes through the group.

"We need to find out how magic works here, and how much is needed to send us home." Amber suggests, and she finishes Willow's braid.

"And what it means to be a fae's mate, how we work out who the portal was *supposed* to drag through."

"Why does it matter who?" Willow asks. "It's not like any of us are going to *stay*."

She has a point.

"Right, I am off to explore, and maybe find someone who can point me toward something I can *smoke*."

With that, Willow rises from the cushioned floor and heads for the wide-open door, bangles jangling and patchwork skirt swishing.

"Want me to do yours?" Amber asks Charlotte, gesturing to her hair.

"If you don't mind…"

"Keeping my hands busy is stopping me from getting stressed out about this whole situation."

Charlotte smiles excitedly and scoots in front of Amber, pulling her hair free of a hair band and leaning back, sighing happily as Amber finger combs her honeyed locks.

I drag a book over from the pile that Alana and Riley have accumulated and start sifting through the pages, in search of anything that will help us get out of Ethea.

Chapter 12

High Lord

My sister is waiting for me when I enter my study. A good job too, as it saves me from tracking her down.

"This just arrived for you," she informs me, holding up an ivory envelope.

I take the letter from her and open it silently. She stays draped in *my* chair, looking bored, while she twirls one of her thick brown curls around her finger.

"Good, the High Lord of Summer Court has agreed to host five of the humans. He's expecting them by the end of the week. With our brother detained, you will need to escort them."

"I have other plans." She brushes me off.

"Cancel them."

"I can't," she insists.

"Then I assume you will be happy to run things here while *I* escort them to Summer Court."

She glares at me then, a look that would have a lesser fae on their knees, but I simply tilt my head in challenge. Her features twitch with frustration and she runs her tongue along her teeth.

"Fine."

I bob my head in forced appreciation. "You should dine with us tonight. Get to know them."

"A generous offer, brother, but I'll pass."

"I think it will do you good."

"I have no interest in getting to know any of the humans. As soon as you release our brother, I expect we will shove them straight back through that portal. It will be bad enough travelling with them to Summer Court. Although admittedly it *has* been a while since I attended one of the High Lord's beach parties."

"And you didn't want to go."

She gives me a sarcastic grin, then rises from my seat. I can almost understand why other fae throw themselves at my sister. Nearly my height, she moves with a fluid grace that is unparalleled. Her thick, dark curls reach nearly to her waist, interrupted only by her delicate high pointed ears and adorned with gold cuffs. Immaculately dressed, as always, she wears colours and cuts of cloth that accentuate her figure. If only she weren't so bitter and lazy.

As she glides across the room to the door, I remember why I wished to see her.

"Sister, one more thing," I wait until she turns back to me before continuing. "The humans need clothing. I will arrange something for the male, but I seem to recall an entire room of unused dresses in your possession. I will send servants to collect them. Be sure to have ten suitably selected when they arrive."

"The servants can select them themselves."

"I would prefer you to do it."

"I'm far too busy to rummage through my old attire in order to dress your new pets."

"*Varian*," I seethe, and she bristles at the sound of her name on my lips, "choose ten dresses from your collection, and have them ready for the servants to distribute in half an hour."

"As you wish, *High Lord*," she snarls before sauntering out of my study.

Fates give me strength. She acts as if assisting me may kill her. It pains me to think about how much my brother usually helps, and that he is currently several storeys below, suffering in iron. But I have passed judgement; I cannot be weak and change my decision.

Slouching in my chair, with my elbows on the table, I rest my forehead in my hands and rub my temples. I will need to speak with the humans, and see if they can arrange among themselves, which of them will stay in Summer Court. They will not be happy about being separated. I dare not admit that I think they will be here for weeks yet. My brother won't re-coup any of his magic while he is in his cell, and even once released, fates only know how long it will take him—and the young Summer Lord—to amass that much magic again. It also hasn't escaped my attention that they cleaved the portal on Samhain, when the veil is at its thinnest. Such an event won't occur again for another six months, and I do not see how I will host even the remaining six humans for that long.

I arrange for servants to go to my sister's chambers, and head for the kitchens to discuss with Cook how we can make our stores last. Although we are technically moving into winter, my court, and the crops it can grow, remain autumnal, and as autumn ebbs, so will the magic that fuels the land. I am already dancing the line of ruin. The prospect of needing to find the additional food, and firewood, and any other supplies the humans might require, fills me with dread.

The magic of Autumn Court cannot sustain such demands for long. Not unless a high born fae finds and claims their mate.

Chapter 13

Seki

As dusk approaches, I put down the fifth book I have leafed through with a huff. So far, we have found nothing of use about fae magic or fae mates. Feeling deflated, I decide to return to my room and have a bath before dinner.

"I'm going to head back to my room for a bit," I tell the others, rising from my scatter cushion. "Keep me posted if you find out anything else?"

Alana nods.

"I'll come with you," Charlotte says following me to the doorway.

I am grateful for her company, especially as she seems to know her way around, and easily navigates our way through the palace.

"It's intense, isn't it?" she asks, as we turn onto yet another corridor. "All these people."

"I'm not so bothered. A bath is what I really want, as I still smell like cake batter."

"Oh… I don't really spend a lot of time around

people. I'm more of a homebody. Being sociable for too long gets me stressed."

"Well, at least you have your own room now that you can retreat to when things get too much."

Charlotte gives me a weak smile as we round the corner onto the 'human hallway'.

"No, absolutely-the-fuck-not!"

I glance at charlotte who looks just as confused as me, before Alex comes storming out of the room she is sharing with Yasmin, clutching a puff of peach fabric.

"Where is he? I'm going to throttle him!"

"Who?" I ask.

"The High Lord."

She shakes the ball of tulle at us, her usually pale face red with anger, then storms down the hall.

"If that fairy bastard thinks he's putting a ginger lesbian in a fucking orange dress, he's got another thing coming!"

A soft giggle draws my attention back, and I find Yasmin stood in the doorway, draped in a stunning copper coloured dress that perfectly complements the warm light brown tone of her skin. Long sleeves grace her slender arms, and a wide neckline shows off her delicate collarbone. The fabric gathers over her bust, drawn in just below with intricate golden embroidery, then falls to the floor in a waterfall of metallic autumnal colours.

"Wow, you look like a goddess," Charlotte compliments.

"Thank you," Yasmin replies quietly, touching her fingers to her lips then extending her back turned hand towards us.

She smiles at us, her cheeks darkening, then closes the door to her room.

"Did the High Lord get us all dresses?" Charlotte asks excitedly.

"I don't know."

We scurry down the hall and when Charlotte opens her bedroom door, she squeals and quickly closes it behind her—eager to try her new dress on, I assume. I continue on to my room, full of curiosity, and there, laid out on my bed, is a swathe of mossy green fabric. I close my door behind me and wander over to inspect it.

I hold it up, admiring the soft, supple fabric, which shimmers in the light seeping through the window. A square neckline, billowing sleeves and a hem decorated with gold and copper stitchwork, embellished with tiny glass beads. It's exquisite and easily be the fanciest dress I'll have ever worn.

Not wishing to spoil it with cake smell, I decide to bathe before I try it on. The bathroom attached to my room is five times bigger than the one in my apartment; spacious, light, and welcoming. I don't know how the fae have managed plumbing, but I am glad they have as I twist the tap and fill the tub. When the bath is full of steaming, fragrant water, I step in, releasing a sigh as I emerge myself.

As I twirl my finger in the water, I wonder if the dresses from the High Lord come at a price. Are they a favour that will need to be repaid? So far, he has fed us, housed us, and clothed us, making no demands, yet I can't help but speculate how long fae hospitality lasts.

My mind wanders back to our conversation in the garden this morning, when the High Lord seemed willing to discuss things more openly with me, without making a deal. If I can get him alone again, maybe I can get him to tell me more about magic and mates.

The only problem with thinking about the High Lord is that whenever I do, I come over all flustered. My pulse quickens and my temperature rises, as I recall how his hair cascaded over his broad shoulders, beckoning to be touched, and how his eyes burned into me with such intensity it set my blood on fire. Even when he was being infuriating, that sensation wouldn't go away.

I release a sigh and slide further into the water, which does nothing to ease the ache I'm feeling. Before, it was just my skin that felt hot and tight. But now it's everything; my breathing feels laboured and my whole body is throbbing.

Without thinking, I reach my hand down between my legs. I slide my fingers through the manicured thatch of fine hair, parting myself and finding my swollen clit. A soft moan escapes me as I circle my fingers around the sensitive bud. My eyes drift shut, and my head falls back against the rim of the tub. I lick my lips because my mouth has dried out, as I continue to pant, circling, circling. I'm close already, so close, so I quicken the pace, chasing my release. My moans turn needy as my whole body tightens, and I conjure the image if *his* heated gaze on me, those russet eyes like molten copper. I stifle my cry as I come, squeezing my thighs around my own fingers as pleasure explodes through my body, from the tips of my toes to the top of my head. I tremble, rippling the surrounding water, as the waves of my release slowly ebb, and my body slackens.

What the fuck is wrong with me?

Chapter 14

High Lord

I arrived at the dining hall far too early, far too eager, and now sit by myself awaiting the humans. After the conversation with my sister and Cook, two of the females accosted me; first the blue-haired one, Willow, came and asked me for herbs to smoke. That was a simple request to satisfy; I sent her to find the gardener, who could advise her which herbs would be safe for her to smoke. Next, the orange haired female, Alexis, stormed into my study, very unhappy with the dress gifted to her. She explained she was a… leziban… whatever that is, and that she found the notion of wearing a dress insulting. Again, it was an easy fix; I allowed her to select whatever she wanted from my brother's collection, as his build is closer to hers than my own. That seemed enough to satisfy her, and she left me in peace. After that, I completed the rest of my daily tasks before returning to my chambers and attempting to make myself presentable.

Chatter from the hallway that leads to the dining hall

alerts me to the human's arrival. I try to sit as nonchalantly as I can, leaning on the arm of my chair, wine glass already in hand and a bored expression on my face.

Seki is the fourth person to enter, and my heart nearly leaps from my chest. She is resplendent in Autumn Court green, gliding into the room as if she were a fate personified.

As the humans take their seats, I notice one is missing, Charlotte. I would ask where she is, but if she does not wish to join us, then that is her business. When all the humans are sitting, I raise my glass and bob my head to them, indicating that they may start their meal.

I spend the entire meal trying not to stare at my mate. She talks and laughs with her companions, and my fae hearing picks up the sound of her voice, as if my ears were made to hear it. The sound is sweet and enchanting, like a birdsong at dawn. I force myself to eat, despite my stomach being tangled, and focus on keeping my breathing steady. I am grateful that she is not fae, else surely she would hear the relentless rhythm of my heartbeat.

Conversations between the humans seem to flow much more simply than conversations with the fae. They are happy to ask one another questions and answer them without hesitation. Each of them seems keen to learn something from the others and show no fear that the information they divulge may be used against them. Strange. They are far more trusting than the fae.

The evening drags by as the humans dine and converse. I eat, but I do not talk. I am not included in their conversations, which suits me fine. My fae hearing allows me to listen to all the discussions occurring, though many of them are on topics I do not understand.

Eventually, the humans filter away. Some head back to their rooms in the south wing and others wander in various directions, not yet ready for bed. Anticipation prickles my skin, as I watch Seki, wondering if she will retire to her room, or if she will explore the palace once more, and I will be able to speak with her. It isn't long before my question is answered.

Chapter 15

Seki

The High Lord has sat at the end of the table all evening and not spoken a word. I have avoided his stare as best I can, but every time I look in his direction, his chestnut eyes meet mine and I flush. Maybe it's the thick fabric of my dress, or the hearty meal, or maybe it is his burning gaze, but I have not been able to cool down all night. Shifting in my seat, and gulping down water as if I have spent the last few days in the desert, I just hope that no one has noticed how out of sorts I am.

As the others leave, I dare a glance back to the head of the table, and he is once again watching me intently, and heat rushes to my cheeks… and between my thighs. *Fuck.*

"Are you coming?" Alana asks as she rises from the table.

"Um… no, I… I think I'll take a walk to cool down before I call it a night."

She smiles at me, then hurries after Alex and Riley, who could be twins with their red hair and matching forest green suits. Only Mollie and Sascha remain, engrossed in conversation at the far end of the table, so with a swallow I stand and head towards the hallway, pleased that I remember which corridor leads to the gardens.

As soon as I step outside, I sigh, then suck in a deep breath, willing myself to cool down, as the crisp evening air tickles my skin. There is a gentle breeze that drifts through the gardens and carries with it a pleasant floral scent. Gravel crunches underfoot as I follow the path along the side of the palace until I round a corner and am met with a stretching lawn. I cross the grass, which is soft beneath my feet, until I reach a stone wall made of pillars carved to mimic trees. Beyond the wall, acres of forest sprawl into the horizon, halted only once they reach the mountains.

"Autumn Court green suits you."

With a squeal, I turn to see the High Lord crossing the lawn towards me.

"You've got to stop creeping up on me," I complain.

"Perhaps you should be more aware of your surroundings."

I roll my eyes at him, then turn back to the horizon. When he comes to stand beside me, it is like standing beside a radiator. Heat rolls off him in waves, and once again I feel flustered.

"I meant to compliment you, not startle you," he explains.

"You managed both," I inform him, then after a pause, "it is generous of you to lend us these beautiful dresses to wear."

I run a hand over my stomach, feeling the soft fabric, so unlike anything I usually wear.

"They are not on loan. They have been gifted, by my sister."

"Well, your sister is very generous."

The High Lord titters, as if I have said something amusing.

"You humans ask each other a lot of questions and seem quite comfortable answering them."

"It's called conversation."

"I admit, your way seems far less complicated than ours."

"It is," I laugh, "We do not make deals or bargains, we simply… talk, and we use each other's *names*."

He stares out at the horizon beside me, silent for a moment, as if digesting what I have said carefully.

"I wish to have a conversation with you," he tells me quietly.

I glance at him then. He is watching me. The look in his eyes is both cautious and longing. Something about that expression on his face makes my chest ache.

"Will you tell me your name?"

He frowns, rubbing his hand along his short beard. Then shakes his head.

"Names… are not given lightly in Ethea."

"Why not?"

"Because they hold power," he sighs, "if a question is asked, or a command given using our name, then… we must answer or act."

"Is it… binding?"

"There is no punishment for *not* doing as we have been asked, but it goes against our nature. It is a dishonour. So, we avoid it by only giving our names to a select few. Usually, only family and… mates."

"Ah, *mates*."

The High Lord bristles beside me. I know this is a subject he would prefer not to discuss, but I need to know…

"Will you explain how fae mates work? Please."

He stares at me for a long moment before answering, his attention flushing my cheeks.

"Mates are… a blessing from the fates. Two fae destined to meet. Usually at least one of them is highborn, and once they are mated, it's for life."

"But your brother believes his mate is a human?"

"He does. It's… unheard of, but then…"

He trails off, reluctant to continue, but I encourage him, desperate to learn as much as I can. Anything that will help us get home.

"But what?"

After taking a deep breath, he answers.

"There hasn't been a recorded mating bond for several generations now. No high fae has been blessed with a mate for a long time."

"Then how are there still high fae?"

He smirks. "A mating bond is not needed to produce offspring. A fae may enjoy many lovers in their lifetime. My sister and I, for example, have different mothers, but… for a mate, a fae would forsake all others."

It all seems rather pointless to me. Why all the fuss over mates? If the fae are comfortable having many lovers, and if mates aren't required in order to have children, then why bother? But then I realise I am asking this of a culture who refuses to give each other their names, and I shrug it off. There is so much I don't understand about the fae, I doubt I could ever learn it all, even if I were to stay here, which I have absolutely no plans to do. After I have been silent for a while, the High Lord speaks again.

"If you have more questions… you may ask them." He tells me, and there is a new sincerity in his voice. I turn towards him, and he looks at me as if he *wants* me to ask them. Maybe he is enjoying our conversation. I consider how best to ask about magic; if he is willing to answer my questions, then I will keep asking them.

"Do all fae have the same magic abilities?"

He tilts his head, his golden-brown hair shimmering

in the fading sunlight with the movement, and it sets my stomach fluttering.

"No… each fae has a specific magic. Usually unique."

"So, you are the only one with elemental magic?"

"Not elemental, just water..."

With a flick of his wrist, he glances back to the lawn. I gasp and watch in awe as thousands of dew droplets rise from the grass and gather like a sea of shimmering beads. The droplets float towards us and merge into an orb of water between us. Then the ball spins like a fluid crystal for a few moments before the High Lord makes a gesture with his fingers and the water takes shape. The orb flattens, then a swirl of petals flow from the center, until the water resembles a flower.

I can't help myself. I reach out and touch the sculpted water in front of me, and I'm surprised when it holds its form. A giggle escapes me as I poke the water flower and it simply reforms when I withdraw my finger.

"Impressive," I murmur, unable to hide the awe in my voice.

"My ancestors could create tidal waves and redirect rivers, even summon a downpour during a drought. But that was before…"

"Before what?" I ask, still mesmerised by the flower glistening between us.

"Before the magic started to die."

I frown at him, not sure I have heard him right.

"With each generation, the magic weakens. I can *feel* it. The magic in Ethea is fading. Soon there won't be any left."

A flick of his wrist sends the flower spraying back over the lawn, the dew droplets returning, as if they had never been disturbed. He turns back towards me and there is a sadness in his eyes that echoes in me. I shouldn't care. This isn't my realm. What difference should it make to me if the fae have their magic or not? If it weren't for their magic, I wouldn't be stuck here.

The sun falls behind the mountains, casting everything in a golden glow. The High Lord watches me so carefully, searching my face for something, and it is so intense it dries my mouth out. Russet eyes churn as they behold me, and my whole-body flushes when I remember touching myself to those eyes earlier.

It's not uncommon for me to masturbate, but the fact that I did it while thinking of a man I've just met is new. Now that I am thinking about it, my core clenches, and my pulse ratchets. I can't pull my gaze away from him…

"Seki I…" he whispers, taking a step towards me.

Every inch of me is hot and vibrating. I'm powerless to stop myself when my feet take a step forward of their own accord, closing the distance between us. His hand rises to the side of my face, his thumb rubbing along my cheek so gently, it sends a skitter down my spine.

He leans in, his handsome face lowering towards me—or am I leaning towards him? Our lips brush, just a fraction, and I am so full of longing that I'm not sure I'm still breathing. A strong hand curls around to the back of my neck, holding me carefully in place as he presses his lips to mine and my eyes drift shut. His mouth is so warm and inviting that when his tongue dances along the seam of mine, I open for him, welcoming him. His tongue caresses mine and when I kiss him back, a soft groan escapes him.

The sound is my undoing, and I reach for him; one arm sliding around his waist, pulling his firm body flush against mine, the other trailing up his chest, wrapping around the back of his neck and tangling in his thick, long hair. He presses a hand against my lower back as he continues to ravish my mouth and it is my turn to moan.

His lips leave mine, even as I whimper my protest, and he trails kisses along my jaw. Lips brush against my ear. Then he kisses his way down the side of my throat, to the curve of my neck, while all I can do is cling on to him, panting with overwhelming desire.

"Oh Seki," he murmurs against my skin.

I go to whisper his name back but realise I don't know it… I don't know it… I don't even know his name. *What the fuck am I doing?*

I come crashing back to my senses and lurch away from him. Detangling myself from his arms and allowing the cool night air to rush into the space between us. Both of us are still breathing heavily as we stare at each other in the wake of our frenzy.

Russet eyes swirl with emotion; confusion, desire, guilt, and I am suddenly filled with panic. I have to leave. No words come to mind, no excuse or rationale. No apology or complaint. Just the unyielding desire to run. So that's what I do. I turn my back on the High Lord of Autumn Court, and I run away.

Chapter 16

High Lord

I knew telling the humans that half of them would need to stay in the Summer Court was a bad idea. As soon as the words leave my lips, the group gathered around the breakfast table erupts. They voice their opinions to me so easily already, and I am not sure whether to be pleased or offended. All I know is that my ears are ringing.

"You've got to be fucking kidding me?"

"You can't separate us?"

"Ooh, that sounds like fun!"

"How long do we have to stay there for?"

"You can't tell me what to do."

The only two silent humans are Yasmin, who is frantically communicating to Alexis with her hand signals, and Seki… my Seki, who sits watching everyone else, without voicing an opinion of her own. She hasn't spoken a word all morning, hasn't glanced in my direction once. I pray to the fates that she is not one of the five to leave my court.

"I know you have a lot of concerns," I begin, in an attempt to calm them, "I assure you, you will be well taken care of by the High Lord of Summer Court. It is a pleasant place. I'm sure those of you who choose to go will enjoy your stay there."

"Choose?"

"How long will it take to get there?"

"Why can't we all just stay here?"

"Yes, it is a choice. One I hope you can reach amongst yourselves. My courts resources are… limited. As a member of the Summer Court was involved in bringing you through the veil, they have agreed to share the responsibility of hosting you. It would put strain, on any court, to host so many at one time." I admit, my pride bruising.

"As for how long it takes… that depends on your horse-riding skills, but no more than three days. I have arranged for my sister and a handful of guards to accompany you."

"How long must we stay there?"

"Is the way dangerous?"

I sigh, rubbing my beard. I steal a quick glance at Seki, but she remains silent, avoiding my gaze.

"The road has… some slight dangers, but nothing my guards cannot handle, I assure you, you will be safe. And as for how long… I don't know. As long as it takes to summon enough magic to cleave open another portal. But you have my word that you will be called upon, and returned here when the time comes."

The group murmur amongst themselves for a while longer. Some of them seem angry, others concerned, even curious. Only Seki remains silent.

"Well, I'm happy to go," announces Willow, who leans back in her chair with a shrug.

"Me too," adds the human with the long blonde hair, Edith.

"Come on Mol—it'll be fun! Remember the map? The Summer Court palace is on the coast, it will be like having a beach holiday," encourages Sascha.

"*Fine*, I'll go. But I want to be notified the second there are plans to re-open the portal." Mollie snarls at me. I don't have the energy to take offence or explain to her how magic works and that a portal cannot be re-opened. A new one will have to be cleaved. So, I simply nod. Only one more human needs to agree to go and my gaze once more falls upon my mate. She looks around the table, and when her mouth opens as if to speak, my heart thunders in my chest. No, no, no.

"I'll go too."

It is not Seki who has spoken, but Charlotte, and I cannot help the sigh of relief that leaves my chest.

"Very well. I will make arrangements. Be ready to depart at midday."

My sister should be out of bed by then.

Rising from my seat, I leave the humans to further discuss what has been decided. As I pass the threshold, I risk a final glance back and find Seki's dark-eyed gaze on me. I almost stumble. She is so breath-taking, but when I see the uncertainty in her eyes, it cracks my heart, and I continue my departure.

She doesn't know she's my mate; she doesn't even know what being a mate means, I remind myself as I march down the hallways towards my study. Although all I really want to do is return to the human group and steal Seki away, so I have her to myself. Even if it is only to talk. Though I would rather kiss her again. I groan, remembering the feel of her lips against mine, her fingers in my hair, her body pressed against me. My cock hardens, again, at the thought as I burst into my study. Sitting behind my desk, I lean back in my seat and huff. I don't know how to do this. I don't know of a single fae who has been blessed by the fates. There hasn't been a mating bond in centuries, and as far as I know, never between a fae and a human.

I know I should tell her, but how? Would it even make a difference? She has a life, a family. She will never choose to stay here. I cannot expect her to give everything up for a mating bond… for me.

Chapter 17

Seki

"How about this one?" I ask, holding up a small leather-bound journal.

"Nope, we checked that one," Riley informs me.

Alana, Amber, Riley and I sit in a circle in the library, continuing our research. We have all returned to our 'human' clothing, which miraculously got washed, dried and returned to us overnight. The only one who chose to stay in their 'fae' attire is Willow, who has been swishing about in her golden-ochre gown all morning, and was last seen practically skipping into the garden, clutching a small bag of herbs and a wooden pipe.

"Here, try this one." Alana suggests, handing me a hefty volume.

I flick through the pages, scanning the words for something useful, my eyes now trained to look for words like 'mate', 'fate' and 'magic'. But nothing jumps out at me. I haven't told anyone what happened last night. No one knows I kissed the High Lord. I keep trying to think of ways to admit it, because I need to tell the group what

I learnt in the conversation beforehand. But every time I cast my mind back, I feel his lips running down my neck, and his warm, firm hand on my back, and I get all hot and bothered again, squirming in my jeans, trying to relieve the throbbing ache between my legs.

"Oh, guys, listen to this," Alana says, scooting further towards us, "Court magic… A court's magic is fuelled by the ruling fae family. Each High Lord or Lady that is chosen to rule a court usually has the aid of multiple siblings, to ensure the magic is sufficient to *maintain* their court, especially in a time of deficiency."

"Deficiency?" Amber asks.

"I haven't seen any magic since we have been here," Riley admits. "Have you?"

"No," Alana answers.

I just shake my head. I don't want to admit that I have seen the High Lord manipulate water twice.

"Maybe the fae are currently in some sort of magical drought. Didn't the High Lord say that Autumn Court's resources were limited?"

I think back to the conversation I had with him last night, when he said 'the magic was dying', that it was somehow fading with each generation. Maybe they're right, and it's some sort of drought, but the way he said it made it feel… bigger… he'd said it had been going on for generations, and that the magic of all of Ethea was almost gone.

I hear Willow before I see her, the sound of her jangling bangles precedes her. A second later she glides into the room, a bag crossed over her body, with an excited gleam in her eyes. As she gets closer, an earthy scent fills the air, and when I look up at her, I notice her dilated pupils.

"We're leaving for Summer Court," she informs us.

We rise from our scatter cushions and follow her out into the lobby, where the other four are waiting. They are all dressed in their 'human' clothes, apart from Willow, of course, and each carries a small bag, supplies for the journey, I assume.

Goodbyes make me uncomfortable, even when I *know* the person I am saying it to. I have only known this group for three days, so making a fuss feels odd for me. Amber, however, sniffs beside me, even as Riley wraps a comforting arm around her shoulder.

"I've never ridden a horse before," Charlotte says, her voice full of uncertainty.

"Oh, it's easy!" Willow tells her. "I learned how to ride a horse when I was volunteering at a ranch in the mid-west one summer. I'll help you!"

We follow the group out into the courtyard where a dozen guards wait, along with a female fae, the High Lords sister I assume, who doesn't even glance in our direction, boredom clear on her elegant face, and a small wagon laden with supplies. Glancing to my right, I spot the High Lord discussing something with the guard, and as if sensing my presence, his head turns and his eyes find me instantly, pinning me to the spot. My breath shudders and I glance away.

"I can do it myself!" Mollie snaps as a guard tries to assist her into a saddle.

The guard backs away with a nod of his head, while Mollie grabs the pommel and, rather unceremoniously, hoists herself up onto the horse. She turns and gives Sascha, who sits atop the next horse along, a satisfied smirk. Sascha just giggles.

Unease gnaws in my gut as the group begins toward the gate. I don't like the idea of us being separated. What if the High Lord amasses enough magic to send us home? We will have to wait days for the rest of the group to return.

Once the convoy snakes through the gate and disappears, I turn to what remains of our group. Riley is still comforting a sniffing Amber. Yasmin is signing quickly to Alexis, who looks confused, and keeps glancing back towards the gate, while Alana is already making her way back into the palace, no doubt heading back to the library. I decide to follow her.

Amber and Riley don't return to the library, it is just Alana and I for the rest of the afternoon as we sift through mountains of books, looking for any clues that might help us get home. Hours drag by, as we seem to find everything but. We find books on botanicals listing the plant life that grows in each court, a guide to 'creatures of the courts' which lists a variety of animals, some of which are terrifying, that live in each court and how to manage them. We also find a bunch of cookbooks, which spark my interest for a moment, until I force myself to refocus. I find a history of each court, with its ruling families, that one at least listed mates but specified little about them.

"I think I have something," Alana tells me, as I skim over a page detailing how the borders of each court were drawn. "This reads more like a mythology book, it's about the fates, but listen to this: 'The fates, knowers of all things both before and beyond, may bestow upon a fae the blessing of a mate. The two are bound, heart to heart, by a golden thread, which only the fates know how to spin. Upon meeting a mate, the fae will feel the thread tighten, drawing them ever closer. The bond will shudder and shake, the magic of the match pulsing, until one fae claims the other'…"

I stare at Alana, unable to speak, my mind reeling.

"Seki, you don't think—"

"No," I whisper, cutting her off before she can tell me what I already know.

She frowns at me, clearly remembering the conversation we had on that first day. When I first laid eyes on the High Lord and felt… *shit.*

I stand, my legs wobbling beneath me, and without a word, head for the door. My feet know the way and I march down the hallway towards his office, my heart thundering in my ears. I don't even knock when I reach the door, I just storm right in.

The High Lord looks up from his desk, a surprised joy on his face, which I ignore and unleash my fury.

"You KNEW!" I scream, and the smile on his face vanishes. "You knew, this whole time, you knew, and you said nothing!"

"Seki I—"

"No! You don't get to talk! You lied to me!"

"I didn't lie, I—"

"You could have told me, at any point, what this was, what this thread, this bond meant, but you kept me in the dark!"

He stands and steps around the table heading towards me, and I step back, my heart pounding so loud I can barely hear myself. I ignore the flush of heat that sweeps over my skin as he steps closer, the way my breath catches in my lungs, and the way I throb between my legs.

"Seki, please—" he begs, reaching out a hand to me.

"No! Don't touch me!" I yell, and he looks at me as if I have struck him. "You had no right to withhold that information from me, *no right!*"

Angry tears roll down my cheeks and I'm pleased when I see how it pains the fae male stood in front of me. His russet eyes churn with anguish, and I stamp down the growing sense of longing that I have for him. It's not real, it's just some bullshit fae magic. I take another step back, increasing the distance between us.

"I want you to stay away from me," I tell him, my voice wavering, my lip trembling, "Stay away from me, until you and your asshole brother find a way to send me *home!*"

Chapter 18

High Lord

I watch my mate storm from my study, and it feels as if my heart is shattering. Stunned, I cannot move. Her words have pinned me to the spot. With each step she takes, the ache in my chest increases unbearably and I shake as panic seeps in, replaying her words in my mind; *Don't touch me, I want you to stay away from me... send me home.* The reality of the situation washes over me, and I realise what a mess I have made.

Could I have acted any differently? Should I have told her straight away? Surely it would have been worse to tell her that first moment in the woods, when I nearly fell from my horse from the shock of finding her. Until three days ago, she didn't know fae, or magic, or mates, even existed.

I suppose I thought over time I could introduce her to the idea… once she had come to terms with fae and magic. Maybe once she had been here a while, waiting to be sent home, she would have fallen in love with the fae realm… with me.

But now she feels as if I have betrayed her, lied to her even and she holds nothing in her heart towards me but hatred. I cannot bear it. The fates have cursed me, not blessed me, to send me a mate I cannot have, a mate who loathes me. No. No, I can't… I can't give up on her. Maybe if I just explain… explain to her I only kept the truth from her because I was afraid the truth would frighten her away.

I take a step towards the door, cursing myself for not deciding to go after her sooner, when a guard appears at the end of the hall and strides towards me. He halts just past the threshold and hands me a blood smeared letter. My stomach lurches.

Tearing the envelope open, I withdraw the parchment note and read through the message quickly.

Winter Court has attacked one of the border villages to the east.

"Fates," I breathe, "prepare ten men, and my horse. While I'm gone, ensure the remaining humans are kept safe, make sure they are given whatever they need, and don't let any of them leave the grounds. Who knows what else the High Lord of Winter could be up to."

The guard bows his head, then marches away. I feel torn, cleaved in two: Half of me knows I must travel east to the border village immediately, to assist those who have survived the attack. But the other half of me longs to chase after Seki and try to set things right.

I detest the thought of being away from her. Now I have found her, I never want to be apart from her, but… she doesn't want to see me. Not now, maybe never again. Perhaps some time to think about what she has discovered will be for the best. I understand her anger, yet… a tiny part of me hopes that when the shock recedes, she will see why I have acted the way I have and give me the opportunity to explain myself. To apologise. I would apologise, for the first time in my life, for her.

Clenching my jaw, I force myself to get ready for departure. I don't like it, but I think it is for the best to give her time. The border village is less than two days ride; I will make an appearance, offer my help where I can, and return within a week.

I had never hoped that I would be blessed with a mate, never thought that after generations of mate-less fae, that I would be chosen by the fates. I have waited a lifetime to meet her, I can wait a week more to see her again. With the fate's blessing, it will not be too late, I will not have lost my mate forever.

Chapter 19

Seki

I stomp through the palace with such force that it makes my feet ache. My heart pounds so hard that the thump of each heartbeat sounds like a wave crashing in my ears. I storm down the human hallway, desperate for the solitude of my room. When I enter, I slam the door shut behind me so hard it makes the stained-glass window on the other side shudder. I'm shaking with so much furious energy that I don't know what to do with it all.

I pace, back and forth, back and forth, sure I am wearing a hole in the rug, huffing out breath after breath as I try to calm down. On what feels like my hundredth lap, I notice a glass of water sitting on the table, and I am reminded of being impressed as I watched the High Lord fill a glass for me using nothing but magic. Enraged, I swipe the glass with a shriek, sending it crashing to the floor. It smashes, shards of broken glass, and water spraying the floor.

The outburst does nothing to temper my fury,

adrenaline still pulsing through me. I stagger back, clutching at my chest where my heart refuses to slow, until my back hits the wall. In the same instant, all the heated energy is sucked right out of me, and I slump against the wall, sliding to the floor.

I wrap my arms around my legs, as I draw my knees up to rest my forehead on them. Breathing heavily, I sit and wait for my pulse to return to normal, with my eyes closed—as if closing them will stop what I have learned from sinking in.

"Seki?" A female voice sounds through my door with a gentle knock.

"Come in," I reply from my curled-up position against the wall.

Alana's friendly face peeks around the door and when she sees me, she lets out a soft gasp and hurries across the room, followed by Yasmin and Alex.

"We heard you slam your door, then scream, everything ok?" Alex asks, sliding down the wall to sit beside me.

Alana sits in front of me, and Yaz sits between them.

I suck in a deep breath, trying to decide how much to tell them.

"Remember the first day we arrived here, and I asked if you felt that weird thrumming, when the High Lord was around?"

"Yeah," Alana answers, her tone curious.

"Turns out there's a reason I'm the only one who feels it," I swallow before forcing the next words from my mouth. "I'm the High Lords mate."

"What?" Alex demands.

"Yep, that tingling sensation is apparently an indicator that your mate is close by."

"How do you know that?" Yaz asks, her voice soft.

I glance toward her, suddenly feeling guilty.

"Um… I don't know sign language."

"That's ok, I can lip read," she smiles.

"Oh… well… Alana and I were in the library, and we found a book about the *Fates*. I assume they are some kind of gods the fae worship, anyway, it explained the mating bond. It said that the bond is essentially a magic thread that binds two people together, and that it shudders and shakes when you meet your mate, kind of like a magical magnet."

"What did he say when you confronted him?" Alana asks me.

"Nothing, I mean, I didn't give him a chance. I yelled at him, told him to stay the fuck away from me until he and his asshole brother figure out a way to send us home, then stormed out."

"Atta girl!" Alex compliments, while Alana and Yaz look mortified.

"It's fine. I'm his *mate*, remember."

"That doesn't mean you can't piss him off, he's still a High Lord."

I just shrug.

"What are you going to do?" Yaz asks, nervously toying with the beading on the hem of her dress.

"Nothing. It's just some bull shit fae magic. I'm simply going to ignore him and steer clear of him until they can get the portal opened again."

Yaz and Alex exchange concerned looks, then make their excuse to return to their room, leaving me alone with Alana.

"You really think you can just stay cooped up in here until we go home?" she asks, shifting to sit beside me.

"I don't know," I tell her honestly, "but I don't want to be around him."

She nods in understanding but doesn't pressure me with anymore questions.

I don't tell her about the kiss, or the fact he showed me his magic. Or about the surprised, hurt look on his face when I rocked up and started screaming at him. I don't tell her that part of me doesn't want him to stay away.

Chapter 20

High Lord

The border village of Nandra sits nestled in a wide valley on the edge of the Winter Mountains. It looms into view as I lead my guards out of the forest that covers most of my court, and the sight boils my blood.

The crop fields to the north of the village lay in ruin. Already struggling soil bears deep slashes, inflicted by claws. The last harvest for the year lays in tatters. Ploughs lay shattered, fences torn down, and the once neat rows of seasonal vegetables are dappled with blood. Scattered amongst the debris, I spot the bludgeoned bodies of half a dozen wraiths left out in the fields for the crows to pick at.

With a sigh, I urge my horse on, my guards following behind me. I am keen to meet with the village Keeper and offer my aid. It has been months since the last attack from the winter court. I had hoped that this close to his season, the High Lord of Winter Court would not strike again until spring.

The attack will have hit my people hard. This was to

be the most bountiful harvest of the year, in the prime of our season. I pray that what they have reaped so far this year will be enough. But I know it won't be. Each year, the harvest is less and less successful, as the land slowly dies, bereft of the magic it needs to flourish. How many more years can my court survive until there isn't enough magic left to feed its people, to keep them safe?

When I was a boy, my father would tell me that when he was young, his father would hold feasts during the autumn festival. People from all over Ethea would travel to Autumn Court for food and drink, music and dancing, and the tables would be laden with food, no thought given to what was hoarded in the stores. Such a thing seems fanciful to me. Now my court struggles to provide for eleven newcomers. It may even struggle with the remaining six.

As we enter the Nandra, the townsfolk emerge from their homes. Their faces are stricken with grief and many of them are weeping. Before I have even made it twenty paces, fae approach me, begging for aid. It breaks my heart to see my people so downtrodden.

"I will see all of you in turn," I promise. "I will meet with the Keeper, then I will take an audience in the Great Hall. Tell me of your misfortunes and I will do what I can."

Muttered thanks echo along the street as I make my way to the town square. The Keeper lives in a small cottage attached to the Great Hall, so his property is always easy to find. I dismount my horse and knock on his door. A gruff voice yells 'enter', and I push my way into the small home, leaving my guards outside.

The grizzly older fae sits at a kitchen table, close to a simple fire, while his wife potters at the stove.

"High Lord," he welcomes, standing quickly from his seat.

His wife turns from the stove and they both bow.

"Thank you for coming with such haste."

"Of course."

"I'll fetch you a drink—" the Keeper's wife begins.

"No. Thank you. I would rather hear what has happened."

I gesture to the table and sit opposite the Keeper as he scrubs his scraggy, greying beard.

"They came in the night," he tells me. "A dozen wraiths, black as coal. The Watchers saw them coming, so stark against the snowy mountains. But by the time the bell sounded, and those of us who could fight were out of bed and dressed, the wraiths had already ransacked half the crops. We went after them with whatever we could, forks, axes, blades, and fire, but it was no use. Two farmers have already died, and three are on death's door, waiting to fade at the Healer's cottage."

My stomach churns as I listen.

"We got some of them, High Lord. My boys got two, pinned them to the ground with iron, left them there to die, but some of them escaped, and flew back over the mountains."

"You did well, Keeper."

He bows his head in thanks. I glance over at his wife as she chops vegetables. What I have to say should really only be said in front of the Keeper, but it would be rude to dismiss his wife. I lower my voice, even though I know it won't help; her fae hearing will still likely catch every word.

"I don't need to remind you, Keeper, that the situation is… dire. The magic of the court is already stretched. I wish to help as many as possible but, I worry that the needs of one, may influence how much I may help the rest."

"I understand," the Keeper nods. "I will speak to the folk as they enter the hall. None shall ask for too much."

"You have my thanks."

I bob my head, then stand.

"I am keen to begin, as I am sure the fae of Nandra are keen to be heard. The sooner we begin, the better."

"As you wish, High Lord."

The Keeper rises too and leads me through a door that adjoins his cottage to the Great Hall, and we prepare for the audience. It is a simple setup, with a table placed between me and the townsfolk, with space beside me for a scribe, who will document the requests and the promises I make.

I will give what I can, but that isn't much. Worry roils through me as I try to anticipate what aid will be requested. I have prayed to the Fates countless times to help me lift the suffering of my court, for it to flourish once more. I know of only one way to do it, only one way to return magic to the land in abundance. But I won't ask. I won't ask my mate to help save my people.

Chapter 21

Seki

It took me all of an hour to calm down after screaming at the High Lord. It took me another hour to summon the courage to return to his office and ask the plethora of questions that circled my thoughts mercilessly.

Only, when I returned, he wasn't there.

When he didn't appear at dinner later that evening, or at breakfast the following day, I sought one of his guards. Knowing how fae feel about questions, I instead simply told him I wished to see the High Lord.

"He's not here." The guard told me rather abruptly.

"Well then, I wish to know where he is."

"Nandra, dealing with court matters."

That was three days ago.

Alana found Nandra on the map, having kept a pile of the books she deemed 'useful'. From the looks of it, the village is closer than the Summer Court palace, and the High Lord said that took three days to reach… so he may have only just arrived there. Which means he isn't likely to return any time soon. I sigh. After finally plucking up enough courage to ask him, I was all geared up to get to the bottom of the whole mates thing, and he vanished. I mean, I did tell him I didn't want to see him until he was ready to send me home, but that's beside the point.

"You're moping," Alana teases.

We're sat in the library, again. But it's just us. The others in our group seem to have paired up. Alex and Yasmin are always together, usually in the gardens, signing away to each other. While Amber and Riley tend to stay in their room. The longer it goes on, the longer I suspect Alana may be right and they are hooking up.

"I'm not moping, I'm just impatient."

She giggles and returns to her book.

"Found anything?" I ask.

"No… not on mates, anyway. I've been looking into magic too, trying to see how it's conjured, where it comes from, things like that, but the fae are as secretive about their magic as they are their names by the looks of it."

I raise an eyebrow, my curiosity piqued.

"From what I can tell, all high born fae get some sort of magic. It lays dormant until they come of age at twenty, but even then, they rarely tell anyone. Sometimes a High Lord will declare his magic, so his court knows what type of magic he possesses, but… the others don't," she explains.

"Hmm."

"What do you suppose *our* High Lord's magic is?"

"Umm…"

Alana's jaw drops. "You know! Don't you?"

"Yeah… I don't know if I should tell you. I mean, you just said they kind of keep it a secret."

"So? Tell me, tell me—oh let me guess… can he fly?"

"Haha no."

"Can he… turn people to stone?"

"Nope."

"Oh, come on! Tell me!"

"What if it's a secret—"

"He kept secrets from you about the whole mate thing. I think that gives you the right to spill one of his."

She looks at me, full of excitement and anticipation. I wonder if it will make him angry if I tell her? He didn't tell me not to tell anyone…

"Fine, but you can't tell the others," I concede.

Alana motions, zipping her lips.

"He has water magic."

She frowns before asking, "So, if you're thirsty he can conjure you a drink?"

I laugh. "He actually did that the first day, I told him I didn't want any wine, so he filled a glass of water from thin air."

"That's disappointing."

"It's actually kind of beautiful. The day we all got our dresses, he followed me out into the gardens after dinner, and he pulled all the dew from the grass and sculpted it into a flower."

I smile, remembering how magical that was, and my mind drifts to that kiss, to his hand caressing my cheek—I shake my head, forcing myself to focus.

"He said his ancestors used to be able to create tidal waves and summon rain if there was a drought."

"Ok, that is pretty cool. I'll give him that."

"I'm glad he meets your approval," I tease.

Her expression turns serious. *Uh oh.*

"Have you thought any more about what you're going to do?"

I shake my head, rubbing my forehead.

"No, I still have so many questions. I suppose I'll just have to wait for him to come back."

"I think it's kind of romantic," she muses.

"Romantic?"

"Yeah… it's like the universe has said 'here you go, here is your perfect person'. You don't have to go on a bunch of dates with losers, or question if someone you're interested in likes you too. All the stress is taken away, and they're just… *there.*"

I roll my eyes at her, but I can't help the laugh that surfaces.

"Well, maybe you're the lucky one who's mated to the High Lord's brother, and the one who got us all pulled through that portal in the first place," I taunt.

When she smiles, it doesn't reach her eyes. There's a sadness in them she quickly hides by changing the subject. It plays on my mind though, and I wonder if she's been burnt in the past. If so, I can understand why the idea of a 'perfect partner' chosen for you would be appealing. Maybe a mate isn't such a bad thing.

Chapter 22

High Lord

Being away from my mate for a week was torture. I consider myself a strong fae, even with next to no magic, but not being able to see Seki has been the most acute agony.

My thoughts the entire ride home have been of her. I did what I could in Nandra, with the promise of more aide to follow—which I will arrange promptly—but there was little more to be done, so I decided to return to the palace.

I stride through the familiar halls, tired, dirty, and hungry from traveling. When I enter my study, I find a handful of letters on my desk, awaiting my attention, and I groan. I wish my brother were here to assist me.

A wave of guilt rolls over me. I am subjecting him to the same torture I have just endured myself, only with the added discomfort of an iron cell. I think of him, sat in the darkness, thinking only of his mate, and the agony I am causing him.

Maybe I should—

The door to my study bursts open and Seki enters, panting as if she has rushed to see me.

"You're back," she breathes, and her voice sends a shiver through me. Oh, how I have missed the sound.

"I am," I reply cautiously.

I cannot yet tell if she is here to scream at me again. I hope that is not the case.

"I'm glad you have returned safely."

My heart gives a hopeful thump. *Has she... missed me?*

"I was hoping I could ask you some more questions."

I feel a flicker of disappointment in my chest. Is she only pleased I have returned so I may answer her questions?

Glancing down at the stack of envelopes waiting on my desk, I think of my brother, and wonder if I should release him before his sentence is served. I am also suddenly very aware that it has been nearly three days since I last bathed.

"I will answer any questions you have Seki, however I—"

"Oh! Of course, you just got back, I'll… um…"

"Can you give me an hour?"

She nods.

"There is an orchard, just beyond the pumpkin patch we walked through the other day, its beautiful at sunset. I'll meet you there."

"Alright," she agrees, then twists on her toes and leaves.

It takes every bit of energy I have left not to forego all my other plans and simply follow her.

I decide the letters can wait. I will get to them later today, if not first thing tomorrow.

While I bathe, I consider what to do about my brother. As his High Lord, I should see that his sentence is served in full. But as his brother, I cannot stomach the thought of him suffering. I have yet to learn which female is his mate. Perhaps I should establish that first and speak to her before releasing him.

Deciding that is the wisest choice, I dry myself and change into fresh clothing. Uncharacteristically conscious of choosing a colour and cut that makes the most of my build and skin tone.

It hasn't quite been an hour, but I decide to head to the orchard anyway; there is no harm in being early.

When I arrive, Seki is already waiting for me. She has her back to me, facing the expanse of apple trees before her. The low sun highlights streaks of copper in her ebony hair, and glistens against her maple-red dress.

I wonder momentarily where she got it and consider if perhaps the human women are sharing or trading their clothes, but I quickly brush the thought aside.

Clearing my throat, in an attempt not to startle her, I step up beside my mate. She turns to me, giving me a half smile, and she is so beautiful it makes my chest hurt.

"How was your trip?" she asks and begins to walk between the apple trees.

"Awful," I admit, "I'm pleased to be home."

She simply nods.

I dare not speak, instead I eagerly await her questions. I will tell her anything she wishes to know.

As I follow beside her, my stomach grumbles loudly, and I remember it has been hours since I had breakfast, and even that was meagre. Leaving Seki's side for only a moment, I reach into the branches of the nearest tree and pull two apples loose.

I bite into mine before I have even returned to Seki's side, the sweet apple juice dancing on my tongue. When I offer the other to Seki, she accepts and takes an eager bite. She pulls the apple away from her mouth, her lips glistening, and the sight has me distracted; I want to lick the apple juice from her lips; I want to feel her tongue against mine again…

Concentrate.

"I'm sorry I yelled at you the last time I saw you," she says, looking straight ahead.

"No, it is I who should be sorry," I say, swallowing my pride. "I should have told you everything sooner, but I… I was scared. I was worried if I told you too much—"

"Did you just apologise to me?"

"I did."

"Does that mean you are now in my debt?" there is a slight teasing tone to her question.

"If you wish me to be…"

She smiles, fully this time, and it fills me with such joy that I smile back. I will gladly be indebted to her for that smile alone.

"So, mates…" she begins, thinning her lips and nodding her head slightly, as if afraid to broach the topic. I share the sentiment.

"How about I tell you what I know, and you help me fill in the blanks?" My mate suggests.

"Alright." I agree, my heart already racing.

"The way I understand it, the *Fates* decide on the two people who should be together, and they create a magical connection… a kind of thread that links those two people together. When they find each other, that thread shakes, so they know they have met their mate. Right?"

"Almost. Yes, the Fates decide, and when they do, we consider it a blessing. When mates meet, the bond pulls taut. Some people call it a snap, but it is intended to *tighten* in order to draw the mates to one another."

She takes another bite of her apple and swallows it before responding.

"And then that's it? Those people are mates, no

questions asked? No choice in the matter?"

"There is a choice. There's a… ritual of sorts, to accept the bond. Theoretically, the bond can be rejected, but it has never been done."

"What sort of ritual?" She asks as she gently kicks the scarlet folds of her skirt in front of her.

I take a bite of my apple, to buy self some time before I answer her.

"The mating bond is traditionally accepted during a moment of… intimacy—"

"During sex?"

I can't help but chuckle. "Yes, during sex. There are words that are exchanged in order to accept the bond. The high fae says their name, their court, and who they are claiming as their mate, the other party says their name, their court, and who they *accept* as their mate."

"So, accepting the bond is the only way for me to find out your name?"

I simply smile at her.

"Hmm… I shall let you keep your name for now," she teases.

Little does she know that if she asked me for it, I would gladly tell her my name.

"Alright, so, have sex, exchange words, and then… mates for life?"

We reach the edge of the orchard, and I gesture for us to sit in the tree line. This side of the orchard looks out over a meadow, then it's only forest all the way to the mountains.

Seki sits down, arranging her dress around her legs and hugging her knees, waiting for my reply. I consider whether or not to tell her everything, but the thought vanishes in an instant. She deserves to hear it all.

"There's more… there's… magic involved, too."

"Magic?" She questions cautiously.

I nod. "Yes, when the bond is accepted, a sort of…

exchange takes place."

I consider how to explain it to someone who has no experience with magic. "Do you have puzzles in the human realm?"

"Excuse me?"

"Puzzles? Sheets of thin wood that have images painted or carved upon them, then the wood is cut into pieces and the game is to fit the pieces back together to make an image."

"We have something similar, yes."

"Alright, so a fae's magic is like a puzzle, and each puzzle is made of, say, ten pieces. When a fae comes of age, they can put their puzzle together, but only nine pieces belong to their image. The tenth piece belongs to someone else's puzzle, it belongs to their mate. When a mating bond is accepted, those puzzle pieces are exchanged, and each person's image is complete. A completed puzzle unlocks that fae's magic—"

"Wait, so before the mating bond, your magic is… incomplete?"

"It's a weak, diluted version of what it *could* be."

She frowns as she absorbs what my explanation. "You said, 'the magic in your realm is dying'… is that because there have been no mating bonds for so long?"

I can only nod.

"So, you want a mate to replenish your magic and heal your court?" There is a touch of hurt in her voice.

Shit.

"No… I mean… yes… but," I sigh, frustrated that my words won't flow and try again, "Having access to full magic and for your court to flourish is the wish of all fae. But given the choice between magic or a mate… any fae, high or low born, would trade every kernel of magic, every puzzle piece for a mate. Having that one person who is destined to be by your side, your perfect companion… that is the true blessing."

Seki releases a long sigh and stares out over the meadow. The sun has now reached the mountains, and the snow shimmers under the last few rays of golden light.

As the silence stretches, my fears grow and the air between us thickens, threatening to suffocate me. "Please say something," I beg.

She lets out a long, wavering breath. "I still have questions."

"Then ask them."

When she shakes her head, strands of her inky hair fall across her face, and I ache to tuck it back behind her ear.

"I can't. Not yet. It's… It's a lot to take in. I'm not sure I could handle any more information right now."

"When you are ready, I will answer any questions you have," I promise.

When she turns to face me, her eyes glisten like morning dew, and the sight makes me ache. I ball my fists at my side to stop myself from reaching for her.

"Thank you," she whispers. "It will be dark soon. Maybe we should head back."

I nod and rise, unable to agree with her because I don't want our time together to end.

We begin back through the orchard in silence and my mind races. I try to anticipate her other questions and stamp on my own. I must answer hers first, even though it pains me to have my own unanswered. Will she reject the bond? That thought alone makes my knees feel as if they will buckle.

"Wait," she whispers, and I realise she has stopped.

When I turn, she stands a few paces behind me, the sun setting behind her, casting her in shadow.

"I need to know something."

I step towards her, and she looks up at me, her eyes full of questions. When a gentle breeze blows and tousles her hair, I cannot help myself. My hand rises and I gently tuck the stray strands back into place, my fingers briefly caressing the curve of her dainty human ear.

"Do I feel like this *because* of the bond?"

"Feel what?" I ask, my voice coming out thicker than I expected.

We are so close, barely an inch between us. One deep breath from either of us and we would touch. My whole body vibrates with yearning at the proximity.

"I'm trying to wrap my head around magic and mates and everything else you have told me, but… I can't seem to think straight when I'm around you. Is that all just part of the illusion?"

"There is no illusion Seki, the bond is real—"

"But if we didn't have the bond, would I still…" She looks down at her feet.

Without thinking, I take her chin between my thumb and finger, tipping her head, so she looks at me. My breath catches in my throat; she is so beautiful.

"Would you still what?" The question comes out in a coarse whisper.

Seki's breath shudders. "Would I still want you to kiss me again?"

My heart thunders in my chest as my whole body fills with longing.

"You want me to kiss you?"

I hear her swallow. "Yes," she whispers.

Seki watches me carefully as I lean in to brush my lips against hers. They are as warm and soft as I remember. Her eyes flutter shut when I press my mouth to hers more firmly, my thumb gliding along her jaw, and my body shudders when I feel her hands on my waist. I rest my hand on her shoulder as she breathes deeply, pressing her chest to mine.

When her tongue glides along the seam of my mouth,

I can't help but groan, parting my lips, so our tongues can meet. She tastes like apples.

What started as tender and gentle becomes something more heated as she kisses me more fervently, her hold on me tightening. I take a few steps forwards, guiding her back against the nearest tree.

She releases a small gasp as her back meets bark, and I pin her between my body and the apple tree. Reaching up between us, she slides her hand around the back of my neck, setting my skin on fire, her fingers curling into my hair.

I leave her mouth, kissing my way along her jaw as she sighs against my ear. The delicious sound makes the elongated tips twitch. My already hard cock does the same as it strains against my trousers.

"Seki…" I whisper as I kiss the hollow beneath her ear.

She rolls her hip, pressing against me, eliciting another groan from the back of my throat. As I kiss along the curve of her neck, she shifts against me so one of her legs is between mine and presses her thigh against me. *Fates*.

"Will you let me touch you?" I ask against her soft skin.

"Yes," she breathes, as the hand at my waist slides up my back.

My hand glides along her waist, over her hip, and down her thigh. I claw eagerly at the folds of her skirt, drawing them up her leg until I reveal soft pale flesh. With a flick of my wrist, my hand slips beneath the fabric, and my palm grazes up the outside of her leg. My hand travels higher and as I skim her hip, I discover she isn't wearing any under-things.

I leave her neck and find her mouth again. She eagerly kisses me, her tongue sweeping into my mouth to find mine as her grip on me tightens. I move the hand behind her neck to cup the back of her head so the bark bites into the back of my hand instead. The last thing I want to do is hurt her.

My other hand drops between her legs, caressing the soft skin of her inner thigh. As my hand slides higher, she rolls her hips against me again, the pressure against my cock both torturous and wonderful all at once.

My fingers meet soft slick curls, and I ease them between her folds. I can't help the guttural sound that slips from my lips at how deliciously wet she is. My mate, so wet for me that I nearly spill right then.

I drag my fingers through her silky heat until I skim the little bud nestled at the top. When she moans into my mouth I devour it, drunk on the sounds of her pleasure.

I circle the bud, slow and languid, causing Seki to pant and tremble against me. Her lips leave mine, so she can rest her head against my shoulder. She is as lost in this moment as I am.

Sliding my fingers lower, I find her center, and tease her entrance with the soft pad of my middle finger.

"Please," she begs, and I am happy to oblige.

The raspy cry she makes when I dip my finger slowly into her has my cock leaking. She is so perfect. She presses her thigh against me once more and I can't help but grind my hips against her, desperate for the friction.

I kiss along her neck again, panting my need against her hot skin. As I pump my finger in and out of her, she writhes against me, already chasing her release.

I add another finger, curling them each time I enter, pressing gently against that soft upper wall inside her. She whimpers, and I know I am pleasing her. I would please her every day, all day, if she asked it of me. Duties forsaken, I would dedicate myself solely to her if that were her wish. I would drown in her and be glad for it.

Muscles tighten around my fingers, and she clings to

my shoulders, her body tensing. I feel myself tighten too, as I shudder against her.

"Oh Seki," I groan against the curve of her neck.

My fingers are coated with a fresh wave of wetness, and she cries her release into my shoulder, her core pulsing around my fingers. I keep moving, slow and rhythmically, in time with my rocking hips, to draw every ripple of pleasure from her.

The throbbing ebbs, and she stills. Although I can still feel her heart racing against mine. When I withdraw my fingers, she gives a small whimper of protest and I can't help but grin ear to ear, knowing I have satisfied her.

I pull back slightly, just enough so I can kiss her again, gentle and tender. She releases a soft hum against my lips, and it is the best sound I have ever heard.

"That was…" she breathes.

"Hmm," is my only response as I brush my lips against hers.

When I take a step back, detaching myself from her, and her arms fall back to her sides, the frigid evening air rushes between us. I stifle a wince as it cools the damp patch at the front of my trousers. Already I feel bereft of her warmth. As I withdraw a handkerchief from my pocket to clean my fingers, I can't take my eyes off her.

Her dark, hooded eyes flutter open, and her glazed gaze lands on me. The soft, satisfied smile she gives me makes my heart sing.

Then her expression shifts. Something like guilt darkens it and she glances away. Eyes focused on the dewy grass at her feet, she frowns.

"Seki?"

"I shouldn't have done that."

"Why not?" I ask, unable to conceal the concern in my voice.

"I.. I don't want to give you false hope."

She looks up to meet my eyes. "I haven't made a decision," she confesses.

"I know," I reassure her, tucking a stray strand of hair behind her ear and stroking her cheek with the back of my fingers.

I smile, despite the cracks in my chest. The closer I get to her, the harder I know it will be to say goodbye to her if she chooses to leave. Just the thought of it is agony.

"Allow me to walk you back to your room."

She gives me a weak smile, adjusting her skirt and pushing away from the tree. If she notices the damp patch, she says nothing.

We begin towards the palace in silence, though my mind fills with a thousand questions, and I bite my tongue. I could talk to her for hours. Conversations with her are so different from those I have with fae. I never want our time together to end.

As we pass into the vegetable garden Seki finally speaks. "I wanted to thank you… for answering all my questions."

I nod, unsure how to respond. When I glance sideways at her, I notice her lip quirk as she considers what to say next.

"I feel like there is so much I need to know before I can even consider what to do."

"I will answer any of your questions, Seki. Anything you need to know to help you make your decision."

"And what if I decide to leave?"

My heart stutters in my chest.

Leave?

"Seki, I cannot force you to stay, it… it has to be your choice."

"I have that choice?" She asks, as if she expects me to keep her here against her will. What sort of male would I be if I did that? I shake my head, disappointed that she could think me capable of such a thing.

"Of course you have a choice," I sigh as we cross into the palace.

Our evening together will shortly end. I wonder if she is any closer to a decision. Does she ask if I would let her leave, because that is still what she would rather do? I swallow the lump in my throat, I would let her go if that was what she wanted… but it would break me.

We round the corner onto the human's hallway, and walk slowly towards the very end, where the door to Seki's room awaits. She slows as we approach, then turns to face me. Her expression is wrought with concern.

"Thank you," I begin, before she can speak, "as always, I enjoyed your company tonight."

Her expression softens. "I enjoyed yours too."

I smile at her then, pleased to hear she enjoys my company. That's a good sign… I hope. Her eyes study my features for a moment, and when she finds whatever she is searching for, she reaches out and caresses my cheek. Her fingers tickle against the short hairs of my beard, and her touch makes my knees weak. Before I can speak, she rises on her toes, her lips caressing mine.

I am momentarily stunned. The air sucked from my lungs. When I come to my senses, I reach for her waist to pull her closer. But I am too late. She lowers herself back to the ground and withdraws her hand from my cheek.

"Good night… High Lord," she bids me, her voice soft and… affectionate?

"Goodnight…" is all I manage, before she enters her room and closes the door behind her, with one last glance at me through the crack, before it shuts.

I don't know how long I stand there, simply staring at the oak door before me. I wonder if Seki is just beyond it, barely out of arms reach, but feeling a world away.

Knowing I cannot stand here all evening, I turn and pace back down the corridor, heading for my own chambers. Not that I am likely to get any sleep. My mind races with possibilities so quickly that it makes me dizzy.

The only anchor I have in the world is her, my mate, and she may yet choose to leave.

Chapter 23

Seki

I am a fucking idiot.

Why did I have to make out with him in the orchard? Why did I have to let him touch me like that? And why was he so damn good with his fingers?

I huff out a breath as I sit at the dresser, dragging a brush through my hair. I have the biggest bags under my eyes. No surprise, really, considering I barely slept.

I had tossed and turned all night, unable to switch my brain off, and then when I drifted off, I had stupidly filthy dreams. My mated subconscious is constantly horny, it would seem. Just as I am wondering if there is any way of getting my hands on—or even making—some concealer, there's a knock at my door.

"Come in!"

Alana pokes her head through the door, then waltzes into the room, followed by Yaz and Alex.

"We were worried about you," Alana begins, "You didn't come down to dinner last night… I didn't want to disturb you last night in case… well… are you ok?"

"Yeah," I sigh.

Alex sits on my bed, raising an eyebrow at me. Yaz sits beside her, a look of concern on her face.

"I'm assuming you spoke to him?" Yaz asks.

I simply nod.

"Well, come on, spill. What did he say?" Alex pokes.

I give them a watered-down version of our conversation, using the High Lord's puzzle analogy and leaving out what we did against that tree.

"Well shit," Alex huffs, "so he only wants to claim you as his mate, so he gets his full magic? That's a dick move."

"I don't think it's like that," I explain, fully aware that I am defending him. "The way he said it… it was like the magic part was secondary… like a bonus or something."

"You're considering it, aren't you?" Alana demands.

"I… I don't know."

"You're kidding right? He's an asshole," scoffs Alex.

"Just because he tried to put you in a dress, doesn't make him as asshole Lex," Yaz teases.

"It does in my book." She huffs, repeating what we have said with sign language to Yaz, who giggles.

"Don't you want to go *home*?" Yaz asks.

"Yeah, of course I do, it's just…"

I sigh and rub my forehead. How can I tell them I enjoy his company? That I can't stop thinking about him? That when I close my eyes, all I see is that look in his—like I'm the best thing since sliced bread. No one has ever looked at me like that, no one has ever made my toes curl with just a glance, or made me come so hard…

"It's complicated."

"I think you're crazy for even considering this, Sek. You should stick to your guns. Tell the High Lord to fuck off and keep your distance until they figure out a way to send us home."

I shrug at Alex's advice, not sure what to say, and let the silence stretch between us.

"My tummy's grumbling. Can we go get breakfast?" Yaz asks.

Alex signs what I assume is 'yes' to her and they both stand and head for the door.

"I'm not hungry," I tell them.

More like I can't face the High Lord right now, despite how much my stomach complains.

"Suit yourself," Alex says as she and Yaz leave the room.

"What's up with *her*?" I ask Alana.

"I don't know. She's been weird for the last few days. Probably getting homesick or something."

I nod, even though I don't feel the same. I consider what I have to go home to and don't find myself feeling sick at all. The only person in my life really is my mum. But when she calls, which is rare, it's only to give me a hard time for dropping out of college and not having a 'real job'. I don't really have any friends, I'm closer to Alana, who I have only known for a couple of weeks, than anyone back home. My apartment is a shithole and the same size as my room here. I'm up to my eyeballs in debt from opening and trying to keep my bakery running, as I barely make enough to cover expenses and pay my essentials. The week before we all got sucked here, I'd eaten sachet noodles three nights in a row because that was all I could afford.

"For what it's worth," Alana interrupts my thoughts quietly, "I don't think it would be so bad to stay here…"

"You don't?"

"No," she shakes her head, "I read a lot… I have always dreamed of being whisked off to a magical realm, and now I live in one… if I had a fae *mate*, and they were nice… I'm not sure I would return home."

"You don't have anyone or anything to go home to?"

She shakes her head ruefully. "Nope… I have little luck with dating, and I don't have any family… not really… I mean I like my job, but that's a pretty boring reason to go back," she giggles.

I nod, my mind now racing with indecision.

"Sure you don't want to come down for breakfast?" Alana asks, pushing her glasses up her nose.

"No… I don't want to face him right now."

Alana simply nods and heads for the door. "I'll leave you to your thoughts then, but if you want to hash anything out with me, you know where to find me."

"The library?"

"The library," she agrees with a grin.

And then she's gone.

I wander out onto the balcony, looking out over the blanket of orange, red and gold as a light breeze caresses my skin. It really is breath-taking here.

I feel like a ping-pong ball. My two decisions are the rackets, and I am bouncing between the two. On the one hand, I'm a human. I belong in the human realm. It's madness to be even considering staying, especially for a man—a fae I have just met. Even if he is handsome, generous and sets my heart racing whenever he is near. On the other hand, what do I really have to go back to? Would it be so bad to stay here?

Time is different here. There are no clocks or watches. Everything is gauged by the sun, sunrise, sunset, and midday when the sun is at its highest. How much time passes between those three events, I don't know… and it probably changes at different times of the year, so I have no way of knowing how much time passes before there is another knock at my door.

Huffing, I plod across the room, wiggling my toes in the shaggy rug as I cross it. I thought Alana was going to leave me to my thoughts.

My heart stops in my chest when I swing the door

open and reveal the High Lord stood in the hallway. Today he is wearing a chestnut brown suit, which on anyone else would look awful, but on him… it matches the colour of his eyes, complimenting his lightly tanned skin and golden-brown hair. When the corner of his mouth curls up into a half smile, my core tightens.

For fuck's sake.

"You weren't at breakfast," he tells me, as if I didn't know, and nods at the tray in his hands.

I hadn't even noticed he was carrying it.

"Usually you choose fruit for breakfast, occasionally a pastry, so I brought you both... may I come in?"

All I can do is nod, slightly taken aback by how easily he asks me questions now. Stepping aside, I allow him to enter. He walks confidently across the room and places the tray on my bedside table, gesturing for me to eat something. I close the door and head for the bed. Sitting on the edge awkwardly and reaching for the glass of water on the tray. After gulping down half the glass, I reach for an apple and bite into it.

"You are avoiding me," the High Lord says matter-of-factly.

"No…" I protest, "I mean… yes… sort of. Not you specifically. I just… I haven't decided and—"

"Seki," he whispers, coming to stand in front of me. I look at his boots until his finger lifts my chin, so I am looking up at him. His light touch causes my breath to catch in my lungs and my skin to tingle.

"I dislike seeing you troubled. There is no rush; until we find out how to open another portal, you do not need to decide."

The smile he gives me is so warm and genuine, I cannot help but smile back. He releases my chin, and crouches before me so we are eye to eye. "In the meantime, I hoped we could spend some more time together?"

My stupid heart flutters at the thought of it.

"What did you have in mind?"

He looks pensive, but I doubt he is only now considering his options.

"When you first arrived, you told me you owned a bakery. Did you bake because you had to or because you enjoyed it?"

"Because I enjoyed it," I answer honestly.

"Then perhaps we could bake something?"

"We?"

"Well… you, I could assist."

I stifle a giggle. "The High Lord of the Autumn Court wants to spend his morning baking?"

"The High Lord of the Autumn court wants to spend his morning with his…. I wish to spend it with you."

He was going to say 'mate'. A brief flash of guilt fills my stomach, but I push it aside—he wants to spend his morning with me, and that makes me giddy.

"Alright," I agree.

The High Lord beams at me.

"Let me change," I tell him, not wanting to ruin one of the loaned—sorry, *gifted*—dresses. I scurry into the bathroom and quickly change into my 'human' clothes, including my apron, which has been washed and pressed.

I'm still knotting the apron when I leave the bathroom and find the High Lord stood in the middle of the room patiently. He tilts his head at my ensemble.

"I didn't want to ruin my dress… these are my work clothes… I mean, I was baking when the portal opened… these are baking clothes."

"Ah, I see."

He nods his understanding and heads for the door, gesturing for me to lead the way. I head down the human hallway, and he comes to walk beside me.

"I thought, seen as pumpkins are one thing we have

in abundance here, we could bake that… what did you call it, cat-zoo?"

This time I cannot hide my laugh.

"Katsu," I correct, "hmmm, I'm not sure you would have all the right ingredients for that here… do you have: panko, curry powder, turmeric, ginger, coconut oil?" I list off the most unlikely ingredients.

"I do not recognise any of those." The High Lord frowns.

"Not to worry. You don't *bake* katsu, anyway. Besides, it would probably make me homesick."

I consider for a moment. "If you have an abundance of pumpkin, we could make pumpkin pie?"

"We could?"

"Yeah," I agree, then list off all the ingredients we would need. To my surprise, Autumn Court has all of them, even nutmeg.

When we arrive at the kitchens, the High Lord tells all the staff to leave. Cook huffs at his demand but ushers the rest of the staff from the room, closing the door behind them.

The kitchen is enormous. Obviously, as it supplies the food for the entire palace, not that many live there. Only the High Lord, his brother and sister, the remaining humans, and the staff, including guards. As far as I know, at least.

A huge wooden table sits in the center of the room. Behind it is a massive fire, with room for several pots, and a gigantic oven. Along one wall is a workbench, and along the other are numerous cupboards. Pots, pans, and utensils hang from hooks in the wall, and an open doorway in one corner reveals a large pantry.

"Tell me again what you need?" The High Lord asks me, keen to assist.

I list off the ingredients and equipment needed and watch with amusement as he scurries around the kitchen to gather everything for me. Once we have everything, I set him to preparing the pumpkin while I begin the pastry. In truth, my hands are far too warm—my whole body is boiling in his presence—to make pastry, but it is the more complex task, so I take responsibility.

"I was wondering if I might ask you something?" The High Lord ventures after a few minutes.

"Sure."

It seems only fair I answer some of his questions and I brace myself for something difficult.

"I have been thinking about my brother," he begins, not the topic I expected. "It has been two weeks since I sentence him to iron," his voice is tight, "I have a mind to finish his sentence early. His magic will be needed… to open a portal… and the longer he is in iron, the longer it will take to replenish his magic."

"I see," I reply, pressing the pastry into a circular dish and sliding it into the oven. I should really cool it first, but the fae don't have fridges.

"I do not wish to insult any of the humans by ending his sentence early, but… it is in their best interest that he recovers from his imprisonment."

"I agree."

"My only concern is… well… he will want to meet his mate."

Ah.

"Do you know which one of us it is yet?" I ask.

"I do not."

I consider for a moment. Admitting that he wants to release his brother so he can send us home sooner shocks me, and I wonder briefly if he has an ulterior motive, but I quickly brush it aside, as it seems unlikely.

It doesn't surprise me that his brother would be eager to meet his mate. We are all here because he was so desperate to meet her, but I can't imagine any of the others being happy about being singled out as the mate of the High Lord's brother.

"Is there a way you can find out? Speak to your brother, perhaps? I wonder if it might be worth speaking to whoever is his mate first. See how they feel about his release?"

"That is wise," he nods, as he stirs the pumpkin mix.

Well, I have never been called wise before.

"What if, whoever it is, does not wish to meet him?"

"Then I shall have to find a way to keep them apart."

"You would do that?"

He nods. "Of course. As with you, it is a choice. I understand that humans are… different to fae. None of you will be forced to do anything you don't want. Everyone will be allowed to return to the human realm if that's… if that's what they want."

"What will it feel like?" I blurt.

He frowns at me.

"Will the bond break when we go back?"

When I glance at him, I find such hurt in his eyes that I realise what I have said and instantly regret it. "Sorry, that was a cruel question, I shouldn't have asked—"

"No, it's fine," he swallows before continuing, "Honestly, I'm not sure what will happen. When the portal closes, with… one person either side of the veil, it might sever the bond. But I don't know how that would feel. To have it, then to not. Or the bond may remain, stretched between the two realms… I don't imagine either would feel pleasant but… I can't be sure. It may simply disappear as if it never existed."

All I can do is nod.

I slide the pastry base out of the rudimentary oven. It looks done, but with no timers, I do not know for sure, and set it on the counter to cool for a while.

The High Lord is quiet, and it doesn't sit well with me. I feel guilty about my last question.

"So, when you're not baking, what else do you do?

What are the roles of the High Lord?" I ask, trying to lighten the mood.

His lips twitch back into a faint smile, and my heart thumps a little harder.

"I run my court, and do my best to provide for my people, travelling to different villages and towns, to listen to what they need and assist where I can. I negotiate trade with the other courts, except Winter of course. It is my duty to keep my people safe and provide soldiers and guards where I can."

"Sounds like hard work," I muse, realising the weight of responsibility he carries.

"It is, but it's worth it. I will do what I can until my magic fades."

A strange feeling bubbles in my stomach, and I wonder if I could ease the burden of leadership. With his full magic unlocked, would running his court be any easier? I sigh and push the thought away. I can't think about that right now.

The pastry has cooled, so I spoon the pumpkin mix into the middle, spreading it with a spoon, and return it to the oven. I have no way to gauge how long to leave it in there, so I suppose I will have to just check it every so often and judge when it's ready by sight.

"Now we wait," I sigh, wiping my hands down my apron front out of habit. It feels good to be baking again.

The High Lord slumps into a chair and I dare to glance over at him. His cheeks are slightly flushed in the heat of the kitchen and his expensive looking suit is splattered with flour and pumpkin flesh. I can't help but giggle when I notice a smudge of flour on the side of his nose.

When he looks up at me, I tap the side of my nose. "You have flour, here."

He rubs the wrong side of his nose with his still floury fingers and creates a larger smudge on the other side, and I laugh loudly.

"Here," I offer, taking a clean cloth and going to stand in front of him.

I gently wipe the flour from his face, and all the while, he looks up at me as if I am some sort of goddess.

He takes the cloth from me and cleans his hands, without breaking eye contact. My cheeks flush and it has nothing to do with the heat in the kitchen, and everything to do with the intensity of his gaze.

My clothes suddenly feel too tight, and my pulse quickens, yet I can't look away. His bright chestnut eyes pin me to the spot, full of want and hope, adoration, and lust. My core tightens again, and I sigh.

When I go to take a step back, he reaches out and takes my hand, halting my retreat. He brings my hand to his lips and kisses along my knuckles, his beard tickling over my sensitive skin. His thumb rubs over the top of my hand as he turns it, placing a gentle kiss to my palm.

Without thinking, I step forward, sliding the hand he holds under his ear and into his thick golden-brown curls, which look like liquid gold in the bright morning light that leaks into the kitchen.

Placing my other hand on his chest, feeling the rapid pounding of his heart against my palm, I position myself over him, then lower into his lap, straddling him.

Winding my fingers into the hairs at the nape of his neck, I lower my mouth to kiss him, eliciting a soft groan as my lips brush his. His hands snake around my waist, pulling me flush against his chest, and I can already feel his thick arousal pressing against my thigh. I run my tongue against his lower lip until his mouth opens for me, and his tongue comes to meet mine.

I roll my hips, desperate for the friction between my legs. The seam of my jeans rubs tortuously against me, as I angle myself so his erection presses against me in the most delicious, tantalising way.

His kiss deepens, his mouth consuming me, possessing me, and for a moment I forget how to breathe. His tongue massages my own as his hands run up and down my spine, sending electric waves skittering across my skin.

I have never wanted anyone more than I want him at this moment. I am utterly lost in his firm grip on my body, on his mouth claiming mine, on his scent of woods and pumpkin spice.

My mouth leaves his for a moment, to suck in a breath, and it leaves me just as quick in a moan as his mouth finds the curve of my jaw. He kisses the sensitive patch of skin below my ear and the crease of my neck as I cling to his hair and his shoulder, pulling him against my neck as he continues to smother me with hot, lavish kisses.

The hand at his shoulder slides down his torso, his body firm and taut under the soft fabric of his shirt. Lower and lower I slide, until I can reach between my legs, and rub my palm against his erection.

"Fates," he hisses against my shoulder.

Lifting my hand slightly, I find the fastening of his trousers. I want to feel him.

Lace up, interesting.

I tug on the laces, loosening the ties enough to slide my hand into the waistband. My fingers quickly find his cock, and I wrap them around his solid length. He's thick, hard as wood, and throbbing against my palm.

A guttural sound tears from him as he buries his head in the crease of my shoulder.

"Seki," he grits out, voice hoarse and panting.

His hands slide under my shirt, splayed fingers skimming up my bare skin, branding me. My grip on him tightens as I work him, my hand firmly pumping him as I continue to grind my hips.

I curl my fingers into his hair, and gripping tightly, I

pull his head back so I can kiss him again. Hot, desperate kisses that have my core pooling.

I pull away from his mouth, resting my cheek against his as I pant, my lips right beside his ear.

"I want you," I whisper, "I need you inside me."

The sound he makes then can only be described as a growl. He abruptly stands, his grip tight enough on me that I don't move. He drops to his knees and lays me out beneath him in one fluid movement.

I wince at the cold slates against my back, and briefly grimace at what might be on the floor underneath me, but my concerns are quickly forgotten as his mouth lowers to mine and possesses me again.

His hips rock as he thrusts into my hand.

"Seki," he breathes, his hot breath fanning my neck.

Reaching his hand between us, he finds the button and fly of my jeans. The button undoes immediately. In fact, I'm convinced he has torn it off. Then the zip is pulled and his hand dips below the waistband.

Before I can draw a breath and prepare, his fingers find my clit, and he circles it with the perfect amount of pressure that has me panting and chasing my release already.

My head lolls back as he brands kisses up the taut column of my throat.

"No," I manage to breathe, "I want this," I demand, squeezing his cock and he shudders.

"Seki I…" he pants against my neck.

I'm just about to squeeze him again when a familiar smell fills my nose.

Shit.

My hand leaves his erection and I pull his hand away from me. The absence of his touch is almost too much, but I know that smell. I would know it anywhere.

Scrabbling out from under him, a look of pure confusion on his face, I lunge towards the oven, where smoke is already billowing through the cracks.

"Shit," the High Lord mutters behind me.

I grab a cloth from the bench, ready to pull the burning pie from the oven. When I open the door, flames lick at the influx of air that seeps into the oven. With a squeal, I fall back, just as the High Lord curses again.

Before I can do anything else, the flaming pie and the entire oven is doused in water. I spin my head to see the High Lord with his arms outstretched as if had thrown the water himself. Then realise he had. He used his magic to put out the fire.

He's by my side in an instant, cupping my cheek, and turning my face towards his.

"Are you alright?" he asks, his voice tight.

"I'm *fine,*" I smile, still panting.

"You didn't get burnt?"

His gaze travels over my face quickly, looking for injury.

"I'm fine," I insist, pressing my palm to his cheek then kissing him softly.

"The pie, however, did not survive."

He chuckles, the sound deep and sonorous, as it vibrates through my chest and sets my toes curling.

He stands, holding his hand out to me, and when I take it, he hauls me to my feet. When he releases my hand, he reaches for the laces of his trousers, and quickly draws them closed, adjusting his still semi-hard arousal, and tucking in his shirt.

I can't help the pang of disappointment I feel that the moment is over as I zip my jeans back up. The button has indeed been ripped off. Then the reality of what we were about to do hits me and I feel… I expect to feel guilty, but I don't… I still only feel disappointed.

The High Lord takes a step towards me, tucking an unruly strand of hair behind my ear tenderly, his fingers brushing my cheek.

"I have some duties I need to attend to, including speaking with my brother."

"Oh," I say, unable to hide my disappointment.

"I will see you later," he promises, ducking to kiss me softly before leaving the kitchen.

I stand there for a moment in the kitchen alone, feeling strange. His exit felt somehow rushed… had I offended him? I don't know the fae ways of lovemaking. Perhaps I did something wrong?

I resolve to ask him next time I see him, then set to cleaning up the mess in the kitchen. It will be a long afternoon, and an even longer dinner, as I anticipate what we will do when the sun goes down.

Chapter 24

High Lord

I try to remind myself that Seki does not know fae ways as I pace towards the dungeon. What she asked of me, what she wanted… When she had told me she wanted me inside her, I had assumed she wanted my fingers again. But I had been wrong, and part of me is glad the pie caught fire, to halt our interaction, because I'm not sure I would have had it in me to deny her.

The first time we join should be when we accept the bond. I have had plenty of lovers over the years, but laying with your mate is different. It is sacred. Not only that, but if I lay with her… and then she still decides to leave… it would destroy me. I can't do it. Once with Seki will not be enough, and I would rather not torture myself with knowing what it is like to be with her, only to have her torn away. I would rather never know the bliss of losing myself in her entirely.

As I descend into the darkness of the dungeon, I push thoughts of my mate aside. I do not think of what she would feel like bare against me, the sounds she would make as I claim her…

A loud drip echoes through the dungeon, and the scarce candlelight casts eerie shadows in the crevices of stone. As I round the corner to my brother's cell, I suck in a breath.

It has been just over two weeks since his imprisonment, but already he looks awful. His skin is pale, his cheeks gaunt. Huddling against the wall in the far corner, he trembles, and a fissure cracks through my chest. I did this to him.

"Brother," I breathe and when he looks up at me, his usually bright eyes sunken and dull, the fissure deepens.

"A month has not yet passed," he informs me, and I notice the scratches on the wall behind him. All sixteen of them.

"I need to speak with you." I tell him, trying to not let my guilt show in my voice. My guts churn as I behold him. I am still his High Lord, I remind myself. I cannot be lenient on him, simply because he is my brother.

"I wish to know if she is still here first." His voice is a broken whisper.

"She is."

He nods, his face twisting in anguish. I keep my distance from the iron bars, even from across the corridor, I can feel their dulling weight. Like the pressure in the air before a thunderstorm.

"Brother, I have a mind to end your sentence early," his head snaps up and his gaze meets mine, desperation racing across his features. "I wish to discuss the… conditions of your release with your mate first."

Dull eyes the same colour as mine search my face suspiciously.

"That sounds to me like a cruel trick."

"No." I try to will as much honesty as I can into my voice when I add, "I have no desire to trick you, but the situation is complicated."

When his brows furrow, I continue, noticing that I am leaning far more towards candour than usual, and I know it is my mate's doing.

"Your magic will be required to send the humans back. The longer you are down here, the longer it will take to replenish."

"I see." The hurt in my brother's voice in tangible.

"For those who *choose* to return," I add, not wanting to dash my brother's hope entirely.

"I didn't think there would be *any* who wish to stay."

"It is too soon to tell, but I hope that some of them will."

His frown deepens, and I realise too late that I have revealed too much.

"It surprises me to hear you say that. I assumed you would want to send them all back as soon as possible."

I consider for a moment how much to tell him…

"I hope that at least two stay behind, your mate… and mine."

My brother stands and walks slowly toward the iron bars, too close judging by his grimace.

"*Your* mate?" he asks, and I wince at the forgotten etiquette.

I nod slowly.

"So, while I have been down here, sick with iron, deprived of my magic, withheld from my mate, you have been up there pursuing yours," he snarls.

"It's not like that—"

"That's what it sounds like to me—"

"It is your fault they are here in the first place! I couldn't let that go unpunished!"

For a moment, I think he is going to argue with me further. I know what he is thinking; that I should be grateful he found my mate, as well as his own, and I am. But he still tore eleven humans away from their lives, their families, their friends, everything they knew on a selfish whim that could have cost him his life.

Eventually, he stumbles backwards, his back slamming against the wall before he slides down it. His elbows rest on his knees and he buries his head in his hands.

"I need to see her brother… *please*," he begs.

"I still do not know which one is your mate."

His eyes flick up to mine, and when I see tears rolling down his cheeks, it makes me ache with guilt. Chestnut irises churn as a battle clearly rages in his mind while he considers telling me. Eventually he folds. With a nod and a sniff, he describes her.

"Her skin is dark, the colour of rich, fertile soil after it's rained," my brother's words are like a caress, as he closes his eyes and conjures the image of her, "her hair hangs in soft bouncy brown curls past her shoulders, and her eyes shine, like polished bronze."

That narrows it down.

"I need more than that."

He frowns at me, considering what else he might know of her.

"There are two humans, similar to your description. One wears circles of glass in front of her eyes to help her see."

My brother's brow creases further.

"I have not seen her wear such things in any of my visions, but… when she talks, she uses her hands… they dance and twist in front of her…"

Yasmin. "I know of whom you speak."

"Brother, will you… will you tell me about her? I have only seen the briefest of flashes." The desperation in his voice clenches my heart, and I excuse his second question, even though we have made no bargains for them.

"She is… lovely, as beautiful as you have described, quiet and gentle. She uses her hands when she speaks because she does not hear as well as the others; the signs she makes are a type of communication aide."

Joy and sorrow mix on my brother's face. "I wish I knew her name."

"I do. Humans are not protective of their names as we are. She is called Yasmin."

"Yasmin," he repeats, the name a whisper.

"I will speak to her brother, but you must accept whatever she decides."

He nods.

"I just want to see her…"

"Trust me brother, sometimes the more we have, the worse it is. The harder it will be if she chooses to leave."

He looks at me, understanding flickering over his face. He swallows, and stares at the stone floor.

"I will return when I have spoken to her," I tell him, and turn to leave.

"Brother wait!" I turn back to him. "Will you give her a message from me?"

I simply nod. He is clearly weak with iron to ask three questions of me. I decide not to hold them against him.

"Tell her… I'm sorry for dragging her away from everything she knows. Tell her I will make it right. That I only did it because…" his voice cracks, "Because…"

"I'll tell her," I confirm gently.

I leave then, making my way back up the stone steps to the ground floor of the palace. I know what my brother was trying to say; that he was desperate. Desperate to meet his mate, to love her. Desperate to unlock his full magic and help restore the court. So desperate he had not considered the consequences of his actions.

As time passes, I find it harder to be angry with him. What he did was reckless, there is no denying it. But a mate… there is no greater blessing, and had I known of

Seki… if I, instead, had my brother's gift of sight… would I have been able to show restraint, where he failed? I'm not so sure. From the first moment I laid eyes on my Seki, I knew I would do anything for her, break any rule, risk any consequence.

I realise then that I would also cast aside tradition for her. If she truly wishes it, then I will take her to my bed. I will give her whatever she wants, whatever she desires, and when I have given her my everything, heart, body, and soul, I only pray that she does not choose to leave me. For it would be a fate worse than death.

Chapter 25

Seki

Dinner drags.

The others are eating so slowly. It wouldn't irritate me as much if I wasn't so desperate to get the High Lord alone. My skin feels too tight, and I am still flushed (and a little bit wet) from what happened in the kitchen earlier. I press my thighs together and squirm in my seat.

It doesn't help that every time my gaze drifts to my right, he is watching me, his molten copper stare burning into me longingly. I glance away, twirling my spoon in the thick vegetable stew I have barely touched. My stomach already feels like it contains a swarm of butterflies. Adding food to the mix seems like a bad idea.

To my left, Alex signs something quickly to Yasmin, and when she nods, they both stand and head for the gardens.

Finally.

Riley and Amber follow not long after, chuckling their way from the hall. It's nice to hear Amber laughing. I am so used to hearing her cry.

"I'm guessing you're waiting for us to leave so you can get him all to yourself," Alana whispers, nudging me with her elbow.

"Is it that obvious?" I sigh.

"You've been squirming in your seat all night, and barely touched your food… you've got it bad," she winks.

"Oh shut up," I whisper with an embarrassed grin.

"Fine, fine, I'll leave you to it… have fun!"

I swat her arm as she rises from the table with a giggle, then return to stirring my stew, afraid to look over at the High Lord again until I am sure Alana has left the room.

The air feels thick and hot—far too hot. But it could just be the dress I'm wearing; the apricot coloured one that Alexis had a tantrum about. It's a little long on me, but I thought the colour looked good against my pale skin.

I hear the door close, and my heart is in my mouth. My pulse ratchets with anticipation. Finally, I pluck up the courage to look at the High Lord, and with a swallow, I turn to face him.

Of course, his eyes are on me, his gaze full of hunger. Without breaking eye contact, he finishes whatever is in his glass, then stands from his seat. Powerful and confident, he strides towards me, halting once he reaches my side and holds out his hand.

"Come with me," he entreats.

I can only nod, my heart all but leaping from my chest.

When I slide my fingers over his palm, his skin scorching, he takes hold of my hand gently as I rise from my seat. Without a word, he leads me from the dining hall.

We travel down an unfamiliar corridor in silence, the

air between us heavy and electric. I barely notice my surroundings. I'm too focused on the golden-brown curls and broad shoulders leading the way.

At the end of the hallway, he pushes open heavy wooden doors and leads me into a spacious room. *His room.* The furnishings are warm and earthy—just like him—browns, oranges, and greens, accentuated with gold. In the center of the room is an enormous fourposter bed draped in lush russet fabric. Beyond it, double doors open onto a wide balcony overlooking the entire court.

He turns, stepping towards me. His eyes churn with desire as he leans past me, pushing the door closed and locking it. In any other situation, I would be scared, but I am the opposite. I feel safe. Resting his hand on my waist, his other rises and he brushes my cheek with the back of his fingers.

"You are so beautiful," he whispers, his voice deep and thick.

I take a shallow staggered breath and close the distance between us, pressing my body against his and wrapping my arms around his shoulders, rising onto the balls of my feet, and arching my neck.

His mouth collides with mine, stealing away my breath. Hands gliding around me, holding the small of my back and the base of my neck, he pulls me closer. His body is large and firm against me, as is his erection digs into my tummy. As his kiss devours me, my core turns molten, muscles clench around thin air, and I can't help the needy moan that escapes my lips.

When he pulls away, leaving me panting, I open my eyes and find him gazing down at me with feral passion. He glances to the bed, then back to me.

"This is what you want?"

"Yes," I breathe, my lips tingling.

When he nods, something flickers across his face that makes me uneasy. "You don't want to?"

"I do… it's just… traditionally, this would be when the bond is accepted."

"Oh."

"But if this is what you want… I will give you anything."

"I want *you,*" I admit.

"Then you shall have me," he promises, dipping his head to kiss me again.

My heart thunders in my chest as his mouth consumes me and I can barely breathe. My mind tries to focus on what he said; that this is usually the part where I accept the bond, but I can't think straight. His mouth, his body, his scent, it is all so distracting. His entire presence overwhelms me, and my thoughts fog as I lose myself in him.

I reach between us and unbutton his jacket. His mouth doesn't leave mine, as I peel the sides away from him, and he wrestles his arms from the sleeves, tossing the jacket on the floor.

Reaching down, I press my palm against his erection before I work the laces. His mouth pulls away for a moment as he sucks in a breath.

He grits out my name, his voice full of desire, before his lips are back against mine. I push my thumbs under the waistband of his trousers and slide the fabric over his hips. He isn't wearing anything underneath, and as his trousers fall to his ankles, I know I have unleashed his cock, but I dare not look down, not yet.

As he steps out of them, he reaches around me and tugs at the laces down my back. He makes quick work of them and before I can catch my breath; he is peeling the dress away from my shoulders as I tug my arms free. The fabric momentarily gathers at my waist before falling to the floor in a pool of apricot tulle and I am bare before him. He reaches behind him, and tugging on the collar of his shirt, pulls it over his head and discards it along with the rest of our clothes.

I let my eyes drop, as his hands come to rest on my bare shoulders, taking in the broad expanse of his chest, the soft fair curls covering it, and the sculpted muscles below. Every inch of him is toned to perfection, as if he has been entirely carved from wood, smooth and hard, and begging to be touched. I can't help myself. I run a hand from his shoulder, down his chest, fingers resting on his abs, which ripple under my touch. My eyes drop lower, to the pulsing erection between us, his prominent head already beading, and the sight of it makes my mouth water, and my core *throb*. He is breathing just as heavily as I am, and when I look back up at him, he is assessing me with the same heated adoration as I am him.

He kisses me quickly, then leads me by the hand towards his bed. I momentarily admire his broad shoulders, muscular back and tight backside, before he peels back the sheets and clambers into bed. Rolling to face me, he holds the sheets up while I slide in beside him.

I shimmy closer, and he leans over me, tenderly brushing the hair from my face and the way he looks at me…

His expression is so tender and full of… is that love? All this time I had thought it was only lust, but even as I think it, I know that isn't true. The connection between us is real and goes deeper than physical attraction. Acknowledging the fact, only emphasizes that I have been denying it.

He snakes a hand around my waist, his touch sending sparks across my skin, his fingers gently tracing up my spine.

I look at him then, really look at him; the warm russet of his eyes, the thick golden-brown curls that frame his handsome face. His palm skims over my hip and down my thigh, leaving branded skin in its wake. His fingers glide along the inside of my knees, then higher, tickling along my inner thigh. The anticipation makes me tremble.

Unbeckoned, my mind considers the moment I leave this realm to return home. The thought of it… it's as if someone has plunged a knife into my chest. My heart seizes and my eyes water, as I realise I cannot leave him.

"Wait," I whisper, as I wind an arm around his waist and press a palm to his chest, right over his heart. His wandering hand pauses.

"You're right. Our first time together should be when we accept the bond."

His brow furrows as he considers my words. "Seki," there's a strange sort of agonised look on his face. He really was going to forsake tradition for me. "There is no rush. I won't force you to decide—"

"I know," I tell him gently, pressing my palm to his cheek.

I take a deep breath, readying myself to take the leap. "I'm terrified," I confess.

"You needn't be," he soothes, his hand gently caressing my thigh.

I can't help but smile at him. He hasn't realised yet what I am trying to tell him. I quickly kiss him before continuing.

"I'm terrified of *leaving*. I was so sure that's what I wanted, but… I thought about it and… just the thought of leaving you breaks my heart. It's ridiculous. I have known you for little more than a fortnight, but I…" I swallow the lump in my throat as my thumb caresses his cheek. "I want you to claim me," I whisper.

Shock tears across his face. "Don't tease me Seki," he pleads.

"I'm not teasing you," I promise. "I've made my decision."

I plant a gentle kiss to the corner of his mouth as he stares at me, disbelief twisting his handsome face.

"You mean it? You really mean it?"

"I mean it," I confirm, beaming up at him.

"Oh Seki," he breathes, his eyes watering as he leans down to kiss me. "My Seki, my mate."

His mouth leave my lips, trailing along my jaw and peppering every part of me he can reach. My whole body aches with need, and I realise now that it is more than simple lust, it runs so much deeper than that. I need *him*, not just his body, but his heart, his soul, all of him.

"Claim me," I whisper again, and this time he shifts, so he is on top of me. I wrap my legs around his hips, the hand that was on his waist trailing up his back, resting on his shoulder.

"You remember the words?" he asks, gazing down at me, his eyes so full of joy that I think my heart might burst.

I nod. "You tell me your name, your court and that you claim me, then I say my name, my… court… and that I accept you."

"You can just say 'human realm', but yes."

He angles himself, and I feel him nudge at my entrance, and I practically whimper.

"Are you ready?" he asks.

All I can do is nod as I smile up at him. He presses his forehead to mine and I curl my fingers into his hair as he whispers the sacred words to me.

"I, Taylen, of the Autumn Court, claim you Seki, as my mate."

Taylen, his name is Taylen.

"I, Seki, of the human realm, accept you, Taylen, as my mate."

A shuddered breath leaves him, as if I have saved his life.

Then he slides into me. One smooth fluid motion and

he fills me so completely that we both groan in unison. My thighs tighten around his hips, as does my grip in his hair. He withdraws, torturously slowly, almost completely, before plunging back into me. As he rocks his hips against me, I cry out, every thrust sending a wave of pleasure crashing through me.

I feel the muscles in his perfect body rippling as he claims me, and all I can do is cling to him. His hips roll as he pumps in such a perfect rhythm that I am already tightening around him.

As I moan against his shoulder, so overwhelmed by him, I feel it… the bond. That bright golden thread that pulled us together burns brighter than the sun, fusing us together, heart and soul. I feel it alight my body and set me a blaze. The bond has been accepted. We are now mates for life, and the rightness of it overwhelms me.

"Taylen," I rasp, I'm close.

"Seki," he whispers into the crease of my neck, he is too.

Every muscle in my body tightens as my orgasm builds and Taylen holds me firmly as he chases his own. One of his hands is buried in my hair, cupping the back of my head as he rests on his elbow, the other grips my hip as he plunges into me.

As if knowing I am on the edge, about to plummet, his mouth presses to mine, consuming me with a hot, searing kiss. One final thrust and my orgasm crashes through me. Taylen devours my cry as wave after wave of bliss ripples through my body. He pulls his mouth away just in time to groan into my shoulder as his own orgasm seizes him, his body jolting against me as he comes. I hold him tight, stars still flickering in front of my eyes, as we both try to catch our breath.

Time seems to lose meaning as we stay that way, bodies still joined, limbs entangled, breath shaky.

Eventually, Taylen raises his head and gazes down at

me, his eyes still hazy, his breathing still heavy. He brushes hair from my face, absolute adoration softening his features, until something catches his eye and his expression changes to one of shock.

"Seki…"

"What?"

"Your ears…"

My hand flies up to my ear and where there was once a short, rounded human tip, I now have an elongated point. Fae ears.

"I… I'm fae?"

"It would appear so."

Taylen smiles at me, his eyes full of wonder as he tucks a strand of hair carefully behind my newly shaped ears. As his fingers caress the tip, a sudden wave of pleasure shivers through me.

"Oh! They're sensitive!" I gasp.

"They are indeed," he chuckles. The sound rumbles in his chest and reverberates through my own.

Well, that's an unexpected side effect of our bond. I'm too lost in euphoria to think about it right now. My body seems to have lost its shape. I feel like a cloud. For a moment, I let myself drift in the fuzzy warmth of being utterly spent, my eyes fluttering closed.

"Are you tired, my mate?"

"Mmm hmm."

When he withdraws and rolls off me, I can't help but grumble a little in protest.

"You should get some sleep," my mate advises me.

"Shall I stay here?" I ask, even though he is already wrapping his arms around me and pulling me against him.

"If you think I will let my mate sleep anywhere but in my bed, I'm afraid you will be disappointed," he informs me, and I can hear the smirk.

I cuddle into him, his body warm and firm, resting

my cheek on his chest as his arm curls around my shoulders and I place my palm over his heart. I breathe him in, pumpkin spice and forests, and release a low hum of contentment I release.

"Sleep, my Seki," he whispers, caressing my cheek and planting a tender kiss on my forehead. And I do.

Chapter 26

Taylen

I'm not sure how long I sleep, if at all, but the first rays of morning sunlight bleed through the window. The weak light casts my bedchamber in a soft golden light and illuminates the woman curled up beside me.

My mate.

I have a mate… The thought makes my chest swell, and my heart so full, I fear my body can no longer contain it. I watch her as she sleeps, and she is so beautiful she takes my breath away. Truly, I am the most blessed of fae. Dark lashes fan over her cheeks. Elegant, elongated ears poke through her thick inky black tresses, and her soft pink lips part ever so slightly, and I ache to kiss her again.

When she stirs in my arms, I still, holding my breath, not wanting to wake her. She releases a content sigh and nuzzles into me sleepily. I can't help the smile that tugs at the corners of my mouth.

I think back to our first meeting, when I nearly fell from my horse, and I wonder if the fates had planned it that way all along. That my brother was meant to pull her through, too. How else would I have ever met her, or even known she existed? My mind briefly considers a life without her, but I push it away. I don't need to think about that. She's here, warm and soft in my arms. And she's staying.

She stirs again, and this time her dark eyes flutter open. After a moment, her head tilts, and she gazes up at me. The smile she gives me causes my heart to stutter.

"Hi," she whispers.

"Good morning."

I tuck the hair behind her ear, careful to avoid the sensitive tip, then let my hand rest against her cheek.

"How do you feel?" I ask.

"Good… I think… you?"

"Never better," I grin.

She beams at me, then reaches up to feel her ear. "Did you know this would happen?"

"No," I admit.

I glance once more at her ears, pale and pointy, still surprised that the completion of the bond resulted in her being turned fae. "I suppose it was necessary, to ensure we have a similar life span, and so that my magic could fulfil."

My magic. I hadn't even thought about it.

"Did it fulfil?" Seki asks, hope lacing her words.

I reach out with my senses, with my magic, and I can feel it. It ripples below the surface, just under my skin, but also all around me, thickening the air. I cast out further than I ever have before, testing my magics reach. Chuckling, I feel all the way to the boundaries of my court. I lick my lips and try something I have always wanted to attempt.

A few seconds later, rain lashes at the windows. Beside me, Seki gasps, her head snapping up to look at the water droplets pouring over the glass.

"Are you doing that?"

"I am."

She turns to me, her expression full of wonder and excitement. "It worked!" she breathes, "You have your full magic. Enough to help heal your court!"

"*Our* court," I correct gently.

She reaches her hand out and lovingly caresses my jaw. "Our court," she repeats, and I bask in her affection.

Leaning closer, she presses her lips to mine in a gentle, tender kiss. I tighten my grip around her waist and pull her against me. She is still naked, and her soft bare skin against my own stirs my desire. Her small breasts (which up to this point I have not yet given my attention—something I plan to remedy very soon) press against my chest and my cock and ears twitch. I swallow my arousal, trying to ignore it. There will be plenty of time for that.

"How does it feel? Your Magic?" Seki asks as she pulls away.

"Like I can feel water.... I can feel the streams and rivers of my court as if they are the blood in my veins, and I can feel the moisture in the air, and bend it to my will."

A frown draws her dark brows together, and she looks around the room. "Hand me that empty glass," she tilts her head towards the beside table.

I do as she asks, my frown matching hers, as she takes the glass in her hand and stares at it. Concentration hardens her features as she focuses all of her attention on the empty glass.

What is she doing?

I watch her for a moment, confused. After a while, I go to question what she's trying to achieve, but I pause. Water gathers along the inside edges of the glass, and slowly, the glass fills. And I'm not the one doing it.

"Seki?" I ask in disbelief.

"I… I think when I got made fae… some of your magic passed to me. When you described how it felt I… I could feel it too…" she glances at me, shock and excitement mixed on her face.

"I didn't know such a thing was possible…"

She laughs and leans over me, returning the glass to the table.

"Perhaps I have enough to help you heal our court," she suggests, and my chest swells.

She has taken so many changes in her stride and yet already she thinks of how she can help. Truly, I am the most blessed of fae.

"If that is what you wish, my mate."

"Of course! I mean, I'm sure I will have duties now, right?"

"Only if you want them. I won't ask anything of you, but that you are mine."

She beams at me. "I'm all yours," she confirms, kissing me again, "but I'd like to help. This is my home now, I want to do what I can, although… I don't know how."

"Perhaps you can be my human ambassador. You know the humans far better than me," I chuckle.

"Human ambassador, I like that."

She lays her head back down on my chest, fingers swirling in my chest hair. I kiss her forehead and rub my thumb in gentles circles over her shoulder.

"Perhaps your first job as ambassador could be to discuss the matter of my brother's release with the others?" I venture.

"You spoke to him?"

"I did."

"Did he tell you who his mate is?"

"Yasmin," I confirm.

"Hmm… she'll probably be on the fence until Alex shares *her* opinion, at least."

"Which fence?" I ask. I don't think I like the idea of the humans climbing fences. They are more fragile than fae. Seki giggles, and the sound makes my whole-body shiver. I could listen to that sound all day.

"Sorry, it is a human expression. It means to be undecided, as in, there is a decision on either side of the fence and she sits in the middle."

"Ah, I see." I feel a little foolish.

"But I'll speak to her… I'll speak to all of them."

"Thank you."

"I'd like to speak to the others too, the ones who went to Summer Court," Seki tells me as she concentrates on the circles she draws with her fingers.

"You think they will have an opinion on the matter?"

"They will… but… that's not what I want to talk to them about. I want to tell the others about the mating bond…"

"Oh?"

"Well… don't you think it's likely that some of the others could end up being mated?"

"I doubt it."

Her fingers pause, and she presses her hand flat to my chest, her skin soft and warm. "Really? Your brother pulls a bunch of us through, two of which are mated to you and him. That can't be a coincidence."

I consider what she is saying. It echoes my earlier thoughts that the fates intentionally sent her to me when my brother sought his mate. Could it be that some of the other humans are intended as mates too? Perhaps my mate is right. She should inform them all of how the mating bond works. Just in case.

"You are wise, my Seki."

"I'm not sure about that. I just don't want you to have a riot on your hands," she giggles.

"Considerate as well as wise, then."

She chuckles again, and I sigh with pleasure at the

sound. As my eyes study her face; her dark hooded eyes, her small nose, and her invitingly soft lips, I decided it has been too long since I last kissed her.

I lean towards her, gently rolling her onto her back, and press my mouth to hers. A hum rumbles through her appreciatively. Her arms wind around my shoulders, and her fingers slide into my hair. When her tongue dances along the seam of my mouth, I open for her, my tongue eager to meet hers. She pulls me against her, deepening our kiss and her hand comes to the side of my head, caressing my ear. Delicate fingers trace along the outside edge, from the bottom all the way up to the tip. I shudder at the touch.

"Seki," I groan.

"They're sensitive—"

"Very."

"Then I assumed you would find this… pleasurable," she whispers, her fingers stroking up and down the length of my ear.

"*Fates*." It is as if she is stroking my cock, which is now tortuously hard. But I must wait. Last night, I was so eager to claim her that our lovemaking was over much too quickly. I wish to learn her body, explore every inch of her.

I angle my head, brushing my nose against her cheek, until my mouth reaches her ear. "Two can play this game, my mate," I whisper, then slowly run my tongue from lobe to tip.

She shudders beneath me, a strangled squeal escaping her.

"Wait!" she breathes, and I pull away quickly at the alarmed tone of her voice. *Did I hurt her?*

When I glance down at her, worry has twisted her expression, and I am filled with concern.

"Am I going to get pregnant?"

"What?"

"Shit, Taylen, we didn't use protection last night. Am I going to get pregnant and have a fae baby?"

I can't help but laugh. "No, my sweet mate," I gently kiss her, in an attempt to ease her concern, "Fae males take a tonic that prevents such things, until we want to produce offspring."

"Oh."

I feel her relax beneath me and kiss her again.

"Do not be concerned Seki, I want you all to myself for a long time. We can discuss fae babies much later." I promise her, my kisses trailing along the curve of her jaw, and then down the column of her neck.

She hums her pleasure, and the sound vibrates against my lips. Concerns forgotten, she tangles her fingers in my hair again, her other hand resting on my bicep as I kiss lower, seeking her breasts. They are smaller than any others I have encountered. Little mounds of flesh, with pale pert nipples. They are perfect. Everything about Seki is perfect. I kiss every inch of the one closest to me, as my mates breathing quickens, her chest rising and falling against my mouth. Finally, I draw her nipple between my lips, tongue flicking over the sensitive skin.

Seki sighs, arching her back, her body begging me for more. I am happy to oblige, my tongue circling around the hardened tip.

"Oh, Taylen," she moans softly, her grip on my hair tightening.

The sound of my name on her lips makes my cock throb, and I am eager to please her. My mate. My beautiful, perfect mate, who is wise and considerate. The fates truly blessed me when they chose her for me, and I vow to cherish her until my last breath.

Chapter 27

Seki

"Taylen, *please…*" I beg, squirming as his tongue flicks over my clit.

I have only just recovered from my last orgasm, and while it is wonderful to be with someone who is content to spend their morning between my legs, he must have blue balls by now. "Come here," I insist.

"But I have not finished exploring you," Taylen mumbles.

I can't help but giggle. "You do not need to get all your exploring done in one morning."

His tongue pauses mid lick, and then he raises his head. His russet eyes gleaming. "I suppose you are right. Once again, you a very wise, my mate."

I laugh as he wipes his mouth on the back of his hand, and crawls further up the bed so he is on top of me. Resting on one elbow, he caresses my cheek, then lowers for a kiss. I practically purr when his lips meet mine, and I wrap my arms around his neck.

Taylen's cock digs into my thigh, causing my core to

pool and my muscles to clench. I *need* him inside me again.

I roll my hips, grinding against him, and he groans. I do it again, as I pull away and angle my head so my mouth is alongside his ear.

"Please, Taylen, I want you inside me."

"When you say my name like that, my sweet mate, how am I supposed to deny you?"

"You're not," I tell him, rolling my hips one last time before he shifts his body to line up with mine.

I feel his head press against my entrance and the anticipation is killing me. Taylen's lips capture mine in a searing kiss, his tongue plunging into my mouth as his cock plunges into my core.

My euphoric scream is consumed by Taylen's kiss as he rolls his hips, languidly sliding in and out of me. Every nerve in my body is on fire, every thrust sends sparks through my veins.

It isn't long before Taylen tenses above me, and I know he is close. I want him to erupt like I have—multiple times—and pull my mouth from his. I tug his head down to my shoulder, so my mouth is alongside his ear.

"Taylen," I rasp, pouring every drop of desire I can into my voice.

My fingers skim up the outer edge of his ear, and when I reach the tip, I take it between my thumb and finger and give it a gentle pull.

"*Fates*," Taylen hisses as his body jerks.

I cling to him tightly, my thighs clamping around him as my orgasm follows. I moan out his name as he continues to roll his hips, each gentle stroke sending ripple after ripple through my body, until I can't take any more and my body crumples.

Every ounce of energy has been fucked right out of me and I collapse into a Seki shaped puddle.

"Satisfied?" Taylen chuckles.

"Very…" I purr.

Taylen rubs a thumb along my jaw, then dips his head for a quick kiss.

I hum as his lips brush mine, and my body tingles, already eager for another round.

No.

"As much as I would like to stay in bed with you all day, we both have things we need to do," I insist.

"The only duty I am concerned with is satisfying my mate," Taylen informs me, already nuzzling my neck.

So tempting.

"I am more than satisfied," I promise, wriggling out from under him.

When he withdraws, I can't help the whimper that escapes my lips. He rolls away from me, and I gaze in awe at his finely toned body; all tanned skin, and sculpted muscle… perhaps our other duties *can* wait.

"We should bathe first," he suggests.

"I really should speak to the others."

"Be that as it may, you and I both smell like sex," he informs me, rising from the bed.

My cheeks flush, even as I watch him stride around the four-poster towards me. The sight of his naked body makes me weak at the knees, and I wonder if this feeling will fade now we have accepted the bond, or if I will always feel this way around him.

"Come, it won't take long," he promises, and before I can agree, he reaches down and scoops me up into his arms, one arm under my knees, one arm around my shoulders.

I wrap my arms around his neck and give him a quick peck on the cheek as he carries me, grinning, into the bathroom.

He lowers me into the tub, and with a wave of his hand, it fills with perfectly heated water. I wonder if this is a new trick, or something he could do before his magic fulfilled. Straightening, he wanders around the room, gathering soap, sponges, and towels. Satisfied he has everything he needs, he joins me in the tub, pulling me into his arms.

"Will you allow me?" he asks, already lathering up a sponge.

I nod, with a stupidly wide smile, and turn my back to him, so he can start there. As he runs the sponge over my shoulders and down my spine, I decide to test my magic.

Twirling my fingers just above the water, I pull a handful into the air. At first it is just a clumsy ball, but as I focus, I manage to make it take the form of a cube. After the cube, I manage a pyramid, and a cylinder, then try something a little more complicated. After a moment of focus, I force the water into the shape of a flower, the same shape Taylen created that night in the gardens. Finally, in a moment of childishness, I manipulate the water into the shape of a penis.

"Very impressive," Taylen chuckles behind me.

I giggle and lose my focus, the water splashing back into the tub.

His sponge filled hands slide to my front, and he takes extra care, soaping up my breasts. A lean into him, my back against his chest as he washes my front. I soft moan escapes me as the sponge dips below the water and between my legs, but Taylen is being dutiful, and carefully makes sure every inch of me is squeaky clean. When my body is done, he uses a jug, magically filled with water to rinse my hair, massaging some wonderfully fragranced soap into it, then rinses it again. As he pours the last jug over my tilted back head, he uses his fingers to comb through my hair, and when his fingers brush my ears, I shudder.

"I've never been turned on having my hair washed

before," I tell him.

His arms snake around my waist, and he kisses along my shoulder.

"Well, you should know then that I plan many more baths with you, where washing your hair will be the least arousing thing we do."

My toes curl at the thought, but I lean forward and pull away before I get too distracted.

"Your turn," I announce, turning to face him and taking the sponge from his hand.

He smiles and nods, then turns his back to me. Tucking his thick hair over one shoulder, I marvel at the expanse of his muscled back, and press my thighs together before lathering up the sponge. I scrub every inch of him I can reach, focusing on the task, rather than how my body is responding.

"Turn around," I instruct him.

When he does, my stomach somersaults at the sight of him. Not only is he ridiculously handsome, especially all wet and glistening, but he is clearly enjoying this as much as I am, based on his erection. My cheeks flush instantly, and the muscles between my legs clench.

"Not getting shy, are you?" Taylen teases.

I simply shake my head and re-lather my sponge. Working my way from the bottom, focusing on his toes, his feet, his shins, his knees, his thighs… I swallow. The sight of his hard, quivering cock makes my mouth water and my core ache with emptiness. I diligently clean him, trying my hardest not to think about how good he feels inside me. When I glance up at him, his full mouth is twisted into a smirk. He is clearly enjoying seeing me so flustered. So, I decided to turn the tables.

Re-lathering the sponge, I reposition myself, so I am straddling him. His erection rests along the crease of my backside, and what small amount of cleavage I have is right in his eyeline. That wipes the smirk off his face.

I take each arm, scrubbing them both, then work from his lower stomach all the way up his torso and chest, his shoulders and neck, all the while his heavy breathing fanning my chest.

"Head back," I order, reaching for the newly filled jug.

I pour the water over his hair, accidentally letting a little of it slosh onto his face. He blinks quickly, and the water makes his eyelashes look thicker. I reach around and apply what passes for fae shampoo into his hair, massaging it into his thick strands, and fingering his scalp. His eyes flutter shut, and he groans. I feel his cock twitch against my backside. Dare I touch his ears… yes, I do.

My thumb skims the tip just a fraction and he hisses.

"Seki…"

"Oops."

"That was intentional."

I chuckle, refilling the jug and rinsing out the shampoo. Once his hair is free of suds, I set the jug down and turn my attention to him.

His eyes are still closed, his neck and shoulders taut as he leans back. I watch as his throat bobs and eventually his eyes open. Thick golden lashes and molten copper find me, and my heart skips a beat. He is so handsome; I can no longer resist.

I take his face in my hands and press my mouth to his. His hands are on my waist in an instant and his tongue meets mine in a frenzy.

Pressing down on my knees, I lift myself slightly and reach down between us. I take a firm hold of his cock and position him right where I want him.

"Seki…" he pleads, voice full of need.

Without another word, I lower myself, taking all of him in one smooth motion.

"*Fates*," he hisses, as I rise on my knees again, before

plunging back down.

Taylen grips my hips, then grinds his own, taking control. I hold on to his shoulders and roll my hips in time with his thrusts. The friction is incredible, and I am already panting.

"Remember what you did to me earlier?" he asks, and before I can respond, one hand leaves my hip, his fingers curling into my hair, thumb gliding up the outer edge of my ear.

Shit.

As he applies pressure with his thumb, it is as if his thumb is between my legs. I pant and moan, completely lost in the sensation, and before I know it, my orgasm is building.

"Taylen…"

I shatter, consumed with bright white light, like an exploding star, and it is all I can do to cling to him and ride out the waves of euphoria as I clamp around him. He bucks under me a few more times before groaning and finding his own release, his arms tightening around me.

He holds me there as we both recover, his fingers trailing up and down my spine, his hot breath on my neck.

"That wasn't supposed to happen," I whisper once I remember how to speak.

"No, it was not."

"You're a bad influence," I accuse.

"I believe you started it," he informs me playfully.

Pulling away slightly, I rest my hands on his chest, and press a heated kiss to his now swollen lips. Then raise my hips and detach myself from him. He grumbles a protest, but I am already wiping myself down.

I need to get out of the bath, or I will spend all day in his chambers with him.

I clamber out of the tub, ignoring Taylen's heated

gaze, and wrap myself in a towel. I scamper into the next room and hurriedly dry myself off. As I drop the towel and search for my clothes, Taylen appears in the doorway, a towel wrapped obscenely low on his hips.

For fuck's sake.

I turn my back to him and locate my dress in a heap with his clothes at the end of the bed. I wriggle into the soft layers of apricot tulle, and stuff my arms into the sleeves, reaching behind me to tug on the laces.

Warm hands take hold of mine.

"Allow me."

Taylen's fingers replace mine and move deftly up the lacings, drawing the dress closed perfectly around me. Even through the fabric, his touch brands me. When the dress is secured, I turn to face him, and find his heated gaze assessing me.

"Perfect," he whispers, his finger tipping my chin, as he dips his head to kiss me. His lips are soft and gentle, despite the longing I saw in his eyes. I rest my hands on his hips as he sighs, and leans in to whisper, "Don't be too long, my beautiful mate, I need to explore just how sensitive these new fae ears of yours are," and then he *nibbles* on the tip, causing my knees to buckle.

A whimper escapes me and he chuckles. Right now, I want nothing more that to rip that towel off him, and have my way with him again, but I *have* to speak to the others.

His thumb and finger still hold my chin as he pulls away slightly to look down at me again.

"Come and find me in my study when you are through speaking with the humans."

I nod, only because I can't remember how to speak.

"I'll have Cook bring us up something to eat. I'm certain we have missed breakfast."

"Okay," I manage, mesmerised by his swirling russet eyes.

"Thank you, Seki," he whispers, his tone turning serious. I don't think it has anything to do with meeting him in the study, so I frown.

"Thank you for agreeing to stay, for accepting me as your mate."

His reverent words crack my heart. "Taylen, you don't need to thank me for—"

"I do. You have made me happier than I ever thought possible, and you have… you have given me hope."

My heart could burst. I take his face in my hands, even as his thumb rubs along my chin and pull him into a kiss. My lips surge against his as I squeeze my eyes shut, tears rolling down my cheeks. When the kiss ends, he rests his forehead against mine.

"You make me happier than I ever thought possible, too. I'm just sorry it took me so long. As soon as I decided, I knew it was right."

"It doesn't matter how long it took. All that matters now is that you are mine."

"I'm yours," I whisper, unable to hide the swell of affection I feel for my mate.

I lean back, beaming up at him, and find his chestnut eyes glistening. Seriousness forgotten, the air turns into something more… content. Filled with the sensation of wholeness, of completion, I lean in to kiss him one last time.

"I won't be long," I promise as I pull away.

If I don't leave now, I never will. I don't look back as I leave his room, because I know if I do, and I see him standing there in that towel, my resolve will dissolve, and I'll rush back to him. So, I keep walking. One foot in front of the other.

I listen to the soft thump of my silk slippers on the hardwood as I meander through the corridors. Adjusting my still damp hair, I try to tuck in my ears. I will reveal them to the others when the time is right, even though my hair tickles against the tips and makes me tingle. That's going to take some getting used to.

I figure Alana is going to be the easiest person to speak to, so I head for the library. She's bound to be there.

I pause in the doorway because although Alana is exactly where I thought she'd be; she isn't alone. *All* the others are with her, and they look up at me in unison.

"Seki!" Alana squeals and rises from her seat, racing towards me. "Where have you been? We've been worried! You weren't at breakfast, then you weren't in your room!"

"I'm fine, I was with Ta— The High Lord."

A frown passes over her face, but is quickly replaced with a grin.

She knows.

I follow her back to the group and plonk down on a cushion next to Riley.

"Well, I suppose it will be easier to tell you all at once." I hedge. I wasn't prepared for this.

"Tell us what?"

I take a deep breath and decide to just come out with it. There's no point in mincing my words. "I've decided to stay."

"WHAT?"

"You can't be serious."

"Are you fucking kidding me?"

Yasmin signs something frantically to Alex, and Alana stays quiet.

"Has he tricked you?" Alex asks, "Drugged you, glamoured you… blackmailed you?"

"No," I insist, "It's nothing like that. It's my decision."

"Are you sure you've thought this through?" Amber asks me. Her tone, at least, is gentle.

"I have… I wasn't *forced* to decide. In fact, I made it

sooner than I think even he expected me to."

"What about pizza, T.V…" Yazmin asks innocently.

"I'm sure I'll be fine without those things," I laugh.

"You're seriously willing to give your whole life up for a man you just met?"

I sigh, not sure how to explain it so they will understand.

"I know, it's only been two weeks, but… the bond is *real*. It's like… we were made for each other. It sounds ridiculous, I know it does, even to me, but… I knew there was a connection between us. I felt it the first day we arrived here, the moment I saw him. I tried to ignore it, to fight it, but as time went on, it got stronger. Then when I accepted to bond, everything sort of… clicked into place. I don't *want* to leave… I don't want to leave him."

Even as I say the words, a knot forms in my throat. *I'm not leaving him*, I have to remind myself.

"This is crazy," Alex huffs.

"So what, when they re-open the portal, you're just going to stay?" Riley asks, a hint of judgement in his tone.

"Yeah," I nod.

The group is quiet for a moment as they absorb what I have said. It is Alana who breaks the silence.

"What's it like, accepting the bond?"

I can't help but smile.

"It's… magical… I felt it. I felt the connection complete, like a bright light of magic *fused* us together. Nothing has ever felt more… right."

Alana's eyes glaze over, while the others all look at me with disbelief. I decide to plough ahead with everything I need to tell them.

"There were… a couple of side effects."

Eyebrows rise all around me.

"Like?" Riley asks cautiously.

"Well…" I reach up and tuck my hair behind my ear, earning me a round of gasps, "it would seem that when a human accepts the bond, they get made fae."

"What does that even mean?" Alana questions.

"I'm not sure, but I woke up with pointy ears, and he seems to think it means we will have a similar life span, however long that is. I still need to ask him about that."

Riley reaches out to touch my ear and I jerk away.

"No!... You don't want to do that… they're sensitive… like… *really* sensitive," I explain.

"Oh… *ohhhh*," he says, realisation drawing across his face.

"Yeah."

"What else?" Alex inquires.

"His magic fulfilled," I begin, "He now has full access to it and its… strong. Hopefully, it will be enough to begin healing the court."

"That's wonderful!" Alana breathes, and I smile at her. She gets it.

"It is, but that's not all. Remember what I told you about the puzzle… about the exchange?"

Everyone nods.

"Well, as it turns out, when his magic fulfilled, some of it also passed to me. Maybe it's because I was human, and didn't have any of my own, but… yeah…"

"You have magic?" Amber asks, confused.

I nod.

"What kind of magic?"

I consider for a moment if I should tell them. I know the fae are secretive about their magic. Only Alana knows what Taylen's magic—my magic is, and I'm not sure if that is my secret to tell or his. I should check with him first.

"I'm not sure I can say. Fae are pretty secretive over their magic… and since mine is the same as his…"

Alana nods her understanding and Alexis scoffs

while the others just frown at me.

"Speaking of magic…" I might as well get it all out in the open now, "he wants to release his brother."

"What?"

"Why?"

"What does that have to do with magic?"

I sigh. This is going to be tough.

"I don't know what his brother's magic is, but I know it was used to cleave the portal. His and one of the Summer Lords. At the moment, he is imprisoned in an iron cell… that dampens his magic. He won't be able to replenish it until he is released. So… the longer he's behind bars, the longer it's going to take before you can go home."

"Your High Lord can't open the portal using his new fancy magic?" Alexis asks, and I try not to glare at her.

"They all have unique magic… it's his brothers that's needed to open the portal."

"Well then, he needs to be released, so he can replenish, and we can go home." Amber insists.

"It's not as simple as that," I explain.

"Why not?"

"Well… he opened the portal in the first place to meet his mate… if he's released… he's going to want that meeting to take place."

"Fuck what *he* wants," Alexis spits.

"You know who it is?" Alana asks.

I nod, "Yeah."

"Who?" Riley demands, and I try not to look directly at Yasmin, rather scanning the group before I continue.

"I don't think it would be fair for me to just announce it. I want to speak to each of you about it individually."

"So you can convince them to stay?" Alex accuses.

I know I need to choose my next words carefully.

"No… but whoever it is needs to keep an open mind."

"Why?" Yasmin asks, and I'm glad she does. It tells me she might have an open mind to the situation.

"Because a mating bond has never been rejected in all of fae history. The impact of doing that is unknown. If whoever it is chooses to leave, the bond will either break, or stretch between the realms, and that could be… harmful, even painful."

"So you're saying whoever it is… is stuck here?" Amber asks.

"No, I… I don't know."

There's one more thing I need to discuss with them. And I know this will probably be the biggest bombshell, but it has to be said. Already I am eager to return to Taylen. I want nothing more that to seek him out in his study and lose myself in his kisses again. I know it's stupid to be missing him. It probably hasn't even been an hour yet, but…

"There's… one more thing," I begin.

"Fuck's sake…" huffs Alex.

"Oh, man…" Even Alana looks concerned.

"I'm going to speak to the others in Summer Court about this as well, but I think… it seems likely that there could be more than two of us who experience a mating bond."

Everyone is silent. Even Alexis. Yasmin taps her on the shoulder and tries to sign something to her, but she isn't paying attention.

"I'm not listening to any more of this shit," Alex announces and storms from the room. Yasmin follows her.

"You really think more of us might be mates with the fae?" Amber asks.

"I don't know," I shrug. "The High Lord's brother and his accomplice, only meant to pull one person through… instead, they pulled through eleven. I felt the bond the second I saw him. Even though I didn't know what it was, I still felt it. Who's to say that as we meet more fae, more bonds won't snap into place?"

Amber looks mortified at the idea, while Riley just rolls his eyes.

"I'm not trying to scare anyone, I just… want everyone to be prepared."

The three of them nod.

"Well, I vote for releasing the High Lord's brother. The sooner he replenishes his magic, the sooner we can all go home." Riley announces, standing.

Amber stands too. "I agree. I vote to release him… I'm glad you're happy Seki, truly I am, but I can't stay here. I need to get home as soon as possible."

Her eyes well with tears, and Riley strokes her arm for comfort. I wonder what she needs to get home for. I don't dare ask; if she wanted me to know she would have told me already.

"Come on, let's go get some fresh air," Riley suggests.

Amber nods, links arms with him and they both leave, heading for the gardens. That just leaves me and Alana.

"Well, that was intense," Alana muses.

"Yeah…"

"For what it's worth, I think you did the right thing, accepting the bond, staying here," she admits.

"You do?"

She nods, giving me a half smile. "I think it's romantic."

"I suppose it is," I smile.

"I'm not sure I'm ready to say anything to the others yet… but… I've been considering staying."

"You have?"

"Yeah… It's beautiful here, sure the circumstances of arriving here weren't ideal, but I'm actually kind of enjoying myself. I don't really have a reason to go back…"

"Do you think you might find a mate?" I ask. She seemed keen on the idea when we last spoke about it.

"No, I don't… I don't think the whole 'mates' thing is for me, but that doesn't matter. I haven't decided yet, but I think I could be happy here."

"I admit, it would be nice to not be the only one who stays."

"Do you think whoever is the High Lord's brother's mate will stay?"

"I'm not sure," I answer honestly.

"I assume it isn't me?" There is a hint of sadness in Alana's voice.

"No," I shake my head.

"I didn't think it would be… who is it?"

"I think I should speak to them first," I explain.

Alana just nods, that sadness still in her eyes… does she… want a mate? She sighs and pushes her glasses up her nose.

"Well, I'm sure you are keen to get back to… did he tell you his name?" she asks excitedly.

"He did… but you know I can't tell you."

"Ohhh." She pouts, and I can't help but giggle.

"I'll tell you one thing though… Can you keep a secret?" I ask her, my voice deliberately conspiratorial.

She nods her head quickly, an excited smile tugging at her full lips.

I glance around to make sure no one is looking, then focus my attention on the open window across the room. The pane still holds water droplets from Taylen's rain, and I pull them towards us. The globules of moisture float across the library like tiny beads and I gather them all together right in front of Alana, then manipulate them into the shape of a flower.

"I knew it!" she gasps and reaches out to poke the flower just as I had.

When we both giggle, I lose my concentration and the flower bursts, spraying us both with water and we laugh even harder. I hope Alana stays. I know I told Taylen that none of the humans were my friends when we first arrived, but I would like to think Alana is now… It will be nice to have a friend who stays behind.

A list of all the things I still need to ask Taylen forms in my mind. I need to know about fae lifespans, what it means to be turned fae, and if there is anything else it affects. Speaking to the others is my next job, my responsibility as the human ambassador. I need to speak to everyone individually, especially Yasmin. I don't know how she's going to feel about being the one Taylen's brother wanted to pull through the portal, or how she will react to the bond. Alexis isn't going to be too pleased.

I also need to know what will be involved in sending the others back, how the magic works, and if there is anything I can do to help. I may not want to return to the human realm, but the others are desperate to. There is even a possibility that they won't be able to open the portal again at all.

As I wander down the hall, thinking about what I'm going to say to Yasmin, my mind wanders back to this morning. To those perfect few hours spent in Taylen's bed—my bed. And in the bath. I can't help the grin that tugs at my cheeks and I restrain a girlish giggle. Already I ache to return to him, to kiss him, to hear the deep timbre of his voice, his laugh. I shake my head at the craziness of it all. There is no more denying it; I have well and truly fallen for the High Lord of Autumn Court. But though there is so much I still don't know, I know one thing for certain; even if Taylen's brother can cleave another portal. I'm not going anywhere. I'm staying right here.

With my mate.

Want more Seki and Taylen?
Check out my Patreon for a bonus Honeymoon scene, and more.
https://www.patreon.com/LunaDaye

Acknowledgements

I was not expecting to tell this story. But once the idea came to me, it flew out onto the page. After sharing the story with my incredible Alphas, they encouraged me to let it lose on the world. So here we are!

As always, thank you to my amazing fiancée, Becks. Without you, I would never have had the confidence to follow my dreams. Thank you for listening and always being there for me. I am eternally grateful for all your love and support.

To my alphas; Ally, Gyselle, and Jenni. I couldn't have done it without you. Thank you for being there for me when I got stuck, and for letting me ramble about all the ideas swirling in my head. Thank you for cheering me on and encouraging me.

Thank you to my betas: Adele, and Liberty. Your feedback was invaluable

To my author friends. Special shout out to Aelina and Jordan. Thank you for encouraging me and letting me pick your brains when I got stuck!

To my Tiktok friends. Special shout out to Cassie. Thank you for all your support and encouragement.

To Sarah de Lang, from Moonrosesxart. My awesome cover designer. Thank you for bringing my ideas to life.

To my family and friends. Thank you all, so much,

for believing in me, and supporting me.

To the writers who came before me. There are too many of you to list. But thank you to every author who has put their story out there. You fill my life with magic, adventure, love (and sometime pain!) You have inspired and encouraged me to create stories of my own.

Lastly to my readers. Thank you for taking a chance on an indie author, for your support, and beautiful words of praise.

With all my heart, *thank you.*

If you have enjoyed Fae's Mate, please consider leaving a review, or telling a friend.

ABOUT THE AUTHOR

Luna lives in North Devon, UK and has been writing stories for as long as she can remember. When Luna isn't writing, curled up with a good book or making TikTok videos, she can usually be found playing video games with her fiancée Becks, walking her pug Dexter, or working on one of her many craft projects.

Don't miss out on new releases, sign up to my newsletter!
Lunadaye.com

Printed in Great Britain
by Amazon

27255813R00101